the
garden
guild

ELIZABETH
BROMKE

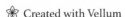 Created with Vellum

For Kathy Bromke

CHAPTER 1—LIL

Sam died on a Tuesday. An uneventful, wet Tuesday in September. Uneventful save for a husband's untimely death, of course. Though even *that* wasn't so... well... *eventful.*

In the room there were four of them, in all, if you still counted Sam, which Lil did for the time being. Sam, Lil, the doctor, the priest. It might have been a punchline in one of Sam's old jokes, if not for the hushed beeping of machines and relentless pattering of rain against the windowpane. And, of course, Sammy's position at death's door.

At fifty, he was too young to die but too old to be considered young. A strange in-between age for a death, no doubt.

A bouquet of red roses sat wilting on the dresser. The baby's breath had lost its white, curdling into a mottled cream color. Despite fresh water and plenty of sun, the once-fragrant get-well gift hadn't even lasted as long as Sam's short coma. It was easy enough to see that there was no saving the bouquet. Much harder to determine such a thing about Sam.

That was the trouble with packaging up dead flowers, Lil knew—they only had so long to carry on. That was probably the trouble with marrying a man like Sam, too.

As for regular old house plants, well, they could be fragile, sure. But they had the soil and the roots and the *potential*.

In fact, next to Sam on the nightstand, Lil's spider ivy thrived, splaying its green leaves like pretty ribbons. The plant was near enough to tickle Sam, it was *bursting* with life in that way. That taunting way.

"Ready," Lil said at last, a shuddering word that almost didn't make its full descent on the room.

Minutes later, it was over. The last rites. The last words. The last kiss on his sallow cheek.

The doctor excused himself, offering tight condolences before dislodging the last of the tubes and mechanisms that had kept Lillian Gulch's husband alive.

Beside Lil stood their priest. An aloof, ancient relic of the church Sam had only ever attended sporadically. Still, he'd shown up. No questions asked. That had to count for something.

Lil walked downstairs after the doctor, her white lace swim cover suddenly itchy. She gave a curt nod to him then scratched beneath the tag at the back of her neck, the sound of nails on her skin too loud. The chilly fall breeze too slick with rain. Everything was just... *overmuch*.

The doctor stepped over the threshold and turned.

"Here you are." He plucked from his coat pocket a rectangular white card. "It's the next step."

Her eyes fell to the lettering, but her head throbbed and tears clouded her vision to the degree that she could scarcely make out the words.

Sniveling briefly, she pushed the pad of her thumb beneath her eyes, smudging blue eyeliner across her cheekbones before studying the card.

Second Street Mortuary.

"Right," she whispered. "The next step."

CHAPTER 2—BETSY

The morning of her forty-fifth birthday, Betsy Borden awoke with a funny feeling. Unable to pin it down, she slipped out from her empty bed and onto the plush carpet, her joints creaking new creaks and her back aching new aches.

Logically, Betsy knew that forty was no different from thirty-nine and indeed not much different from twenty-nine. But Betsy also knew that forty didn't engender its reputation for nothing. As of forty, certain truths crawled out from the cracks of life—the truth about what a woman had made of her life. *Who* she had made it *with*. Or not. What she had to show for four whole decades on earth.

She shrugged at her bedside and her neck kinked up. She muttered a curse, let loose a dramatic sigh and worked the knot with her thumb knuckle.

Once Betsy tugged her silk robe about her, she maneuvered into the pink-trimmed bathroom and pulled her hair this way and that—finally giving up to shower and shampoo, following up with a new cream rinse she'd ordered from a catalogue.

After the shower, she returned to the mirror, unwrapping her towel from her head and taking to the blow dryer with a passion.

Twenty minutes later, her hair fell as fluffy and fresh as possible about her shoulders. She leaned closer to her reflection, studying the lines around her eyes, the two trailing up toward her forehead. Might be time to work on that.

Her gaze danced down toward her jawline, and she pinched the skin there. Jowls? Couldn't be. She gave her face a quick shake.

Nothing.

"Whew," she murmured.

But then...

Something caught her eye. Something far less egregious but far more alarming. A fleck of light. Something that did *not* belong... forty years old or *not*.

A single, crooked white hair.

The offensive fiber shot out not from her temple... not from her springy brunette bangs... but from her *chin*.

Sure, Betsy had had her share of chin hairs. But a *white* one? It meant one of two things: either Betsy was turning into a blonde in her old age. Or, she was turning into a witch.

Never having desired to be a blonde in all her *life*, Betsy prayed for the latter, plucked the hideous shoot, and patted her makeup furiously before storming downstairs.

There, propped against the coffee maker, sat a

birthday card from her mother, Betsy's name written in neat script across the envelope.

"Thank you, Mother!" Betsy called into the front room where she could hear Jane Fonda on the television and her mother sliding across the carpet in tennis shoes, counting to eight.

"Don't thank *me!*" A hoarse voice bellowed back.

Betsy smirked and slid the envelope aside to set the machine.

Her mother, clad in a leopard-print leotard and slack black leggings, emerged with a towel draped about her neck—for show, in all likelihood.

There was no doubt about it, the woman made sixty look better than forty. At least, better than *Betsy's* iteration of forty.

"I *said*—" Her mother stabbed at the card then shook her bejeweled finger. "—don't thank *me.*"

"Let me guess, Ma," Betsy returned, slipping a finger beneath the flap and springing it open. "A Weight Watchers membership."

"I *wish.*"

Betsy frowned as she opened the card—elegant white stationery with a simple *Happy Birthday to my daughter* and *Love, Ma* written within.

"What's this?" Betsy unfolded a single typewritten page that had been taped inside the card.

Her mother shook her head and clicked her tongue.

Betsy returned her stare to the familiar paper, her eyes flicking along her signature. And then, an unfamiliar one. "Book with Borden. It sold. *We sold,*" she whispered gleefully, unbelieving.

Book with Borden was the name of her father's travel agency—a flashy, successful empire of a travel-booking company that John Borden had built from the ground up in the sixties.

When he passed before Betsy was a teenager, Betsy's share of the business was slotted into a trust for her twenty-first birthday. On that day, she entered the world of travel-planning, first slowly, by helping out in the local store. Later, in greater measure by attending board meetings and seminars, participating hand-in-hand with her father's business partner until his death just two years prior. In the time since that death, Betsy learned just how little love she had for the business—or any business whatsoever. She was ready to decompress. To *retire*.

But her mother was *not* ready for Betsy to retire. Especially if it might affect her life of luxury. Which it wouldn't. Not now. Not with the handsome payout.

"I met with the broker yesterday afternoon," Betsy's mother offered mildly. "You were getting your nails done when she called."

"And you didn't tell me?" Betsy's eyes flew to her mother's. "You didn't bother to tell me?"

"I figured I'd save the news for this morning. Happy birthday, Betsy. You got your wish."

Her mother poured a mug of coffee and strolled to the kitchen table, perching on the edge of a chair there and staring meaningfully into the middle distance.

"The girls will be here soon," Betsy warned, disinterested in attending to one of her mother's moods. "Birthday brunch. Remember?"

The woman waved her off. "I'll hide in my room.

Don't worry about me. High time I start looking for an old folks' home anyway."

"Ma." Betsy laughed then moaned and joined her at the table. "An old folks' home? Be serious."

Her mother's face grew solemn. "I *am* being serious. If you care so little about your own independence, then I'd better find a way to protect *mine*."

"That doesn't make any sense, Ma," Betsy reasoned. "We'll have plenty of money to keep you independent. And me, for that matter."

"You are squandering your life, Betsy." She stabbed the table with her red fingernail. "There are women who would *kill* to have your job. Your *company*. Your status. We didn't fight for you to throw it out the window."

"*We*?" Betsy snorted. "Mother, please. As if you were standing there with Susan B. Anthony, on the cutting edge of women's rights."

"Just because I wasn't doesn't mean I value them any less."

"And me selling Book with Borden doesn't mean I value them any less, either." Betsy lowered her voice. "I like my free time. I like my life. I am not going to waste it in marketing meetings and—"

"How will you, then?"

"How will I what?" Betsy adjusted the gold amaryllis brooch on her lapel and returned to the breakfast bar.

"Waste your life?"

Betsy laughed, and the doorbell chimed. The Gull's Landing Garden Guild. Right on time for her birthday brunch. She smoothed her blouse and tweaked a daffodil in the vase on the counter. "With my social circle, of course. And *you*, you know. Maybe I'll take up aerobics, too." She grinned and eyed her mother as she made her way toward the front door. "There are plenty of ways for a woman to keep busy, you know. Plenty of ways for women to *contribute* to society, Ma. Running a company isn't the only one."

CHAPTER 3—EMILY

Emily Addams had found her way to the seaside hamlet of Gull's Landing on little more than a whim, in truth.

After a particularly brutal fight with Jimmy, Emily had packed exactly one suitcase and driven home to her father's house.

Once there, her stepmother had slapped a newspaper and a pen down on the table and instructed her to start hunting.

When Emily asked, "For what?" the cold woman had replied, "Someone else to take you in."

Weepily, Emily had flipped to the classifieds, looking first for a position locally, in Wildwood. All she had in terms of work experience were three months in beauty school, one semester in nursing school, and one year working weekends at a florist's boutique on the board-walk, a job which she'd quit once she had married Jimmy.

In the classifieds, Emily had found three nanny listings, two dental hygienist positions, a teacher's aide gig, and a call for waitresses at the seediest restaurant this side of the Atlantic. Then she saw it: a small box buried in the corner between listings for Rusty Mechanics and the Limecrest Quarry. A funeral home in the town next door —Gull's Landing—had put out for a secretary.

When Emily had called about it, she had learned that not only was the pay a full dollar above minimum wage, but the funeral director also let rooms from his house. Emily had asked if he lived in the funeral home. He'd laughed and said, "No. Four blocks south, actually."

Emily liked that. She liked that things were situated in Gull's Landing according to their distance in blocks. She liked that a kindly-sounding man rented rooms from his family home. She liked, mostly, that Gull's Landing was a world away from her hometown and all its disappointments.

She had given her interview over the phone and then left the next morning.

And now here she was, stepping off the bus at Second Street and Elm. From the bus stop, if her hand-scrawled directions were accurate, she had exactly two blocks until she made it to her first destination of the day: 92 Second Street—the Second Street Mortuary.

Twisting the handles of her bag in her hands, Emily looked right then left as the bus doors wheezed shut behind her, sending the monster off on its way across the Jersey Shore.

It would appear that she stood at the very end of a little main street. Where she stood on Elm was empty, no traffic save for cars parked along a vaguely residential road.

Left and up, she spotted a green street sign that read "Second Street".

Right and down farther, way beyond the bench for the stop, Elm Street was vivisected by a busier thoroughfare. Slow-moving vehicles drove through her view of brick buildings, one on the corner with an umbrella poking out from its side.

Though her sense of direction was wobbly at best, Emily knew that just a few blocks beyond the umbrella and its corner café was the boardwalk and its white sandy beach.

At least, she knew as much from common sense. Emily had never been to Gull's Landing, despite its relatively close proximity. That was the problem with growing up too fast, she suspected. When you grew up too fast, you went exactly nowhere.

And yet Emily had lived many lives in her twenty years. One broken home. Three stepmothers. Countless stepsiblings. Potentially one or two half-siblings, depending on where her mother was and what she was up to. And then Emily's own short adulthood, complete with two marriages. Two humiliating marriages.

The first ended with a blow to her nose.

The second with a blow to his groin.

No one could accuse Emily Addams of not learning from her mistakes. Which was why she was happy to start over.

The warm sun bled down on her and a breeze curled

around her body, tugging her toward the glimpse of activity down the way.

Glancing at her wristwatch—the one thing her mother had left behind—Emily calculated that she did *not* have enough time to stroll down and inspect the cityscape of her new home.

That was just as well, though. She could save it for later. If Emily had learned one thing, it was that there was no rush.

She took to the sidewalk with a purpose, pushing along, carefully avoiding the cracks as she narrowed her focus on the sign for Second Street.

Perhaps the street below, the one with the lolling one-way vehicles and happy noise, was First Street.

That would orient Emily linearly, and she liked that. To slot herself into a grid. It'd be a good change. To fit in somewhere. If only she could. In her life so far, Emily hadn't been very good at fitting in.

Partly, she wished Mr. Grimwood had offered to meet her at the house first. She might like to know where that was before signing her contract. But then, if she went by her instinct about him—that he was a nervous, careful sort—she'd say he'd guessed that she'd feel better meeting in a more public place first. That would allow her to size up this Grimwood character before deciding she could sleep in the same building as him.

Emily shook her head. She really needed to stop trying to climb into the minds of men. She was no good at it. Her instincts were usually wrong.

～

"You must be Miss Addams."

Tall, thin, and dark-haired, Mr. Grimwood was younger than Emily had expected him to be. Though by how much, she couldn't be sure. With a quiet, unassuming character but a professionalism to suggest years in the business, he could be anywhere from thirty-five to fifty, she figured.

"Yes. Emily." She offered a hand. "How do you do?"

"Norman Grimwood." He shook her hand. "We'd better get to it, Miss. I've got a funeral on Saturday."

"Oh, I'm sorry to hear—" Emily started, then gave a short, awkward laugh, remembering that a funeral would be commonplace now. Not necessarily something to mourn over anymore, so to speak.

Mr. Grimwood smiled kindly. "You'll get used to it."

"Excuse me?" She faltered, shifting her bag in her hands. It had grown heavy on her walk, and she suddenly felt strange for having brought just one bag. Strange, perhaps, because it was immediately apparent she *would* be staying. She *would* be working there, at the Second Street Mortuary. She *would* be moving to Gull's Landing.

"Death, I mean. You'll get used to it." As he said it, his smile slipped and he waved over to the receptionist's desk, a heavy wooden piece, barren on top save for a thick leather-bound planning book in the center and, at the very corner, a healthy, vibrant green plant. She eyed the plant, finding comfort in something familiar.

"A peace lily?" She pointed.

Mr. Grimwood cocked his head. "So you do have experience?"

Emily shook her head. "Only with flowers. I worked for a florist before."

"Well, flowers and plants are a big part of what we do here," he replied.

And with that Emily wondered if she would fit in after all.

CHAPTER 4—LIL

Thank goodness for family.

Lil was shrouded not only in black lace, but also in a huddle of relatives as the priest droned on about life after death.

The wake, held in the Gulch family home as was the ritual in the deeply morbid Catholic tradition, had carried on without a hitch.

And now here they were, droves of people, each with some tie to Sam or Lil or both. Usually both. How rare it was for a man or a woman, once married, to have many acquaintances *outside of* the marriage.

At least, that's how it ought to have been.

Even with Lil's coolness over the past week, funeral director Norman Grimwood handled things masterfully.

He and a sweet-faced assistant treated Lil like a queen and Sam like a fallen hero, even though Sam was anything but. Then again, neither Norman nor the girl would have known that. As far as Gull's Landing knew,

Sam was a good-natured good old boy. A union man. A husband. A beach bum.

Indeed, Sam was all of those things. But not a single one could have redeemed him in Lil's eyes.

No, he wasn't a brute. He just had that wandering eye that Lil came to seethe over. He called her jealous, but it wasn't jealousy that had Lil riled up all those days and nights. It was *un*acceptance. Lillian Russo Gulch refused to accept that her husband went bowling until well past midnight. She refused to accept that the receipts she'd discovered—some from Wildwood Bunkhouse, some from Wildberries Burlesque —weren't the precursor to what eventually happened.

And yet none of that meant that she wouldn't mourn him. That she hadn't mourned him. She did.

But the truth about Sam meant something else. It meant that when Norman Grimwood introduced himself with a warm handshake and a soft, dimpled smile, and kind, blue puppy-dog eyes she could get lost in... well, she did. Lil got lost in them.

Norman didn't realize this, probably. After all, grief shielded Lil. Grief despite decades of anger and hurt and discontent. Stupid grief that hadn't earned its spot in Lil's heart. In her life.

But by the time the town car had pulled up to the Second Street Cemetery, a pretty, colorful field that spread behind the mortuary, the grief had ebbed.

The sunglasses and veil helped disguise the truth. Particularly during the burial. They shielded the fact that Lil's tears had long dried.

Once the service had finally concluded and Sam had

been lowered in slow spurts down into the earth, the crowd broke away from the hollow spot, spreading out across the cemetery, unsure if it was safe to slip off into their vehicles for good—leaving Lil to deal with the days and weeks that would stretch thereafter.

It *was* safe, but most of the attendees didn't realize it. At least, not if their lingering behavior was any indication.

Lil waved off her well-meaning relatives and remained in her seat—a metal folding chair hidden beneath a white linen cover.

The others huddled in hushed semi-circles, throwing furtive glances her way. Glances she felt more than saw, since she was trying her hardest to both focus on the casket and the overdone bouquet that lay atop of it *and* also draw the attention of Mr. Grimwood. Norman. She figured if she kept still enough. Quiet enough. Odd-acting enough, he'd break away from the priest and the groundskeeper and see to Lil. See if she needed company there, in her metal seat. Or if she'd need company after. Or if she was *okay*.

No one had asked her that. If she was *okay*.

She figured she was.

But still. It'd be nice if someone just sat next to her and took her hand and said, "Hey, Lil. Are you okay? I bet you've had a hard few days. Maybe you've had a hard few years." For the love of God, she *had*. She really had.

And yet, she was okay.

A sigh slipped through her lips just in time for a breeze to carry it off and pull her gaze to the funeral guests.

Lil spotted her nieces frolicking in a grassy clearing beyond the oak tree where Sam now rested. The joy in her life, those girls. Spending every summer with her. Nagging her. Giving her grief. Giving her trouble and giving her life. Maybe Lil would move to Philly. Be closer to family.

Nah.

Too much work.

Her eyes took in the greater cemetery—the whole of it.

The green rolling hills of the Second Street Mortuary. The neatly tended gravesites. Polished tombstones and gleaming marble offset by some older but still well-kept markers.

She twisted her head and took note of her one friend group—if she could even still call them that—the Gull's Landing Garden Guild.

Lil hadn't been to a meeting in years. *Years.*

But they had shown up. Only one or two did she recognize, and even then... they looked *different.* Like the club had taken on a new task that had more to do with personal upkeep than garden grooming. And if she didn't know any better, it would appear they'd acquired a new member, the likes of whom Lil was none too pleased to spy.

She stood and started for the group, finding a moment to perhaps reemerge. Pay her dues. Confront the interloper, even. But just as she sank one heel into the green tuft of earth, a figure appeared in front of her.

"Mrs. Gulch." Her expression stricken and uneasy,

Norman Grimwood's helper seemed worse off than even Lil.

"Yeah?" Lil cleared her throat and furrowed her brow. "Yes?"

"Hi," she squeaked. "I'm Emily. Emily Addams. Mr. Grimwood's secretary and assistant, and I'm just wondering if you intend to return to the mortuary to collect the flowers *now* or if you'd like for us to deliver them to your home?"

Lil glanced back toward the priest and the funeral director who were chatting quietly together.

"I don't think I'd like to have them at all." The words left her mouth as if they weren't her own. Lil didn't know where such a sentiment even came from. Surely, she'd like the opportunity to have this kind child and the warm Mr. Grimwood over for an iced tea or a hot toddy... if it was later and the night grew cool.

The girl blinked.

Lil ran her tongue over her painted lips then grimaced at the taste, dabbing her mouth beneath her veil with a white handkerchief. "Would the funeral home like to have them? The flowers? Maybe we could spread them out here, across the less-visited graves?"

The girl frowned and fidgeted. "Well, um. I can ask?"

"Lil!" A woman's voice cut through the awkward exchange and Lil looked past the poor, well-meaning little Emily Addams.

"Yes?" Lil didn't recognize the woman, a solidly built brunette. She stood in a fashionable, structured pantsuit. Pointed white and black heels planted on the grass and didn't sink into it, unlike Lil's own heels. It seemed physically impossible that the imposing woman before her floated on the dew-damp sod while Lil, a wisp of a woman, sank.

"We haven't met," the woman bemoaned. "But I'm Betsy Borden, and I am *so* sorry for your loss. You see, I'm the new president of the Gull's Landing Garden Guild, and although I know you've been in and out, I want to invite you for Sunday brunch with us tomorrow. That is, if you aren't hosting family. A distraction can be good in times like this."

Lil frowned at the babbling woman. A distraction *could* be good in times like this. But wasn't this woman overstepping her bounds? Still, something in this Betsy gal rubbed Lil the right way.

"That sounds nice," Lil answered. "Er, but I do have company." Her lips pinched, she looked around the cemetery for her sister-in-law. "And I have to see to the flowers." Lil waved a hand at the girl who stood awkwardly by.

"Do you need help?" the woman asked. "We can help." She hooked a thumb to the staring group of women beyond.

Lil frowned. "I, um, well, I'm not sure." It was wholly unnecessary for Lil to say anything more. All she ought to have said was yes or no and thank you and that was *it*. But she did say more. "You see, I don't really want the flowers. I was just asking the girl here—*Emily*," Lil felt a little glow from recalling her name, "if we could maybe distribute them around the cemetery or—" Lil lifted her hand to gesture to the other graves and, as she did, it shook. Her voice broke and she bent at the waist, drawing her other arm across her abdomen as an unexpected sob crawled out of her chest.

"Mrs. Gulch," the girl dropped to the ground on one side.

"Oh, honey," the woman lowered herself on the other.

Lil couldn't see. Couldn't hear. Couldn't feel.

But an hour later, she was propped up at her kitchen table. A white pill on her tongue, a hot toddy in her hand, and five vases of red roses and white baby's breath—alive and colorful and fresh—lined up on the table in front of her.

CHAPTER 5—BETSY

Betsy held court at the table. There were only four of them in total, and Lillian would make five. *If* she came.

They sat together beneath a bright red-and-white striped umbrella on the patio just outside of Maeve's, a quaint bakery-deli café. The only open table that could accommodate their odd-numbered party had six seats, leaving two open. Nervous for Lillian, Betsy mentally planned for Lillian to take the seat between Betsy and her mother, Lena.

Autumn touched the air and, as such, Betsy had taken care to wear a new sweater—black with red buttons— and cream-colored linen pants. Her dark hair was clipped back in a barrette, her bangs teased, and her red lipstick immovable... so long as she sipped her tea with a straw.

The three other ladies had been reticent about inviting Lillian. Snooty, even. But Betsy wouldn't tolerate that. Lillian was on the books as a dues-paying member, and even if she weren't, it was only right to set something up.

Now, though, it was upon Betsy to rein in the gossip.

"New to town?" one of them whispered loudly across to Betsy, batting her painted eyelashes meaningfully at the next table over.

Betsy slid her gaze to the lone girl seated facing away, her elbows propped on the table, a frumpy flannel shirt hiding her petite figure. Sprigs of wispy blonde hair shot up from a messy ponytail. She was one of those types who could be all of twelve or all of thirty—who was to say?

The Garden Guild had lately turned themselves into the Gull's Landing welcome wagon, nosing their way into every sphere of local life. It was Betsy and her mother, however, who truly led the group. And it was Betsy who could put a squash to the busy-body behavior. Betsy who could encourage new membership. Betsy who had the final say in how the group moved through the seasons.

She dropped her voice. "New hire at the funeral home."

Her mother elbowed into the conversation. "I hear she's from Wildwood."

Betsy lifted the potted orchid from the ground and set it in front of the empty table setting next to her. Lillian's gift. "Ladies," she started, clearing her throat. "Before Lillian arrives, maybe we can discuss our November project."

"I'm out for November. Heading to Florida," Nancy replied, blowing a stream of cigarette smoke off the back of the table and waving the slender stick that was crooked in her fingers with some measure of false elegance. Betsy was no fan of smoking. A formidable, tasteless habit with no more glamor than snapping gum at the dinner table. Betsy was also no fan of Nancy, truth be told.

"I thought we were skipping November," Pam chimed in. "I have company clear through to next month."

"We're skipping *December*," Betsy reminded them. "November is the harvest parade. We always sponsor a float. Goodness, Pam, you *rode* on it last year."

Pam rolled her eyes and unfolded the cloth napkin, smoothing it across her lap before settling her stare upon the white fabric.

Betsy smirked. "All the more reason to recruit new members, I suppose," she huffed. "Well, if you two are out, then I guess it's up to me to—"

"What am I?" Lena Borden cried out. "Chopped liver?"

Nancy and Pam plastered fake smiles across their lips, but neither had much to add.

Betsy eyed the second empty seat, just at the end of the table, complete with a place setting. A setting the waiter, had he been properly trained, would have known to remove when Betsy declared they were a party of four and tentatively expected just one more.

She pursed her lips, ran her tongue over her teeth, and glanced left and right along the sidewalk that stretched down First Street. "Excuse me," she murmured, scooting her chair back, standing, neatly folding her napkin, and laying it across her seat before crossing the brick patio to the girl who sat alone.

"Miss?" Betsy stood at the girl's side, and she could

feel the others' eyes on her. Good. They ought to watch. Ought to see an example of a true Garden Lady, as they used to jokingly refer to themselves after a glass of wine. That was months ago, when the Garden Guild boasted more than four stodgy old cranks. A time after Lillian Gulch had been an active member, apparently. That in-between time when Betsy discovered the club, driving herself into it like a lynchpin, saving the group from falling apart altogether.

The girl paled and shrank. Her eyes darted off beyond Betsy.

"Hi. I'm sorry to bother you, but I'm Betsy. Betsy Borden. The president of the Gull's Landing Garden Guild?" She sang it into a question as though the title might ring a bell for the poor stranger.

"Oh." The girl seemed no more comfortable and much more confused.

Betsy smiled and waved back to the group. "We're having a little brunch for one of our... one of our members. You see, Lillian Gulch—you know the Gulch family from the recent funeral, no doubt—"

The girl twitched, but Betsy couldn't read whether her reaction was unease or not.

"Mrs. Gulch?"

"Yes," Betsy answered, jumping on the opportunity. "Anyway, we'd love for you to join our party over there, if you're so inclined... that is, of course, if you're not expecting someone?" Betsy gestured to the open seat.

The girl blinked at her own table then shifted her gaze over to the other. Betsy followed it to find her mother, Nancy and Pam staring.

She gave them a look in time for the girl to glance away.

"I'm fine, thank you."

"What was your name again?" Betsy pried.

"Mine?"

"Yes. I promise I mean well. I'm sorry if I seem... intrusive, but the Gull's Landing Garden Guild, well, we try to make it our mission to be welcoming. And then, of course, we are always on the hunt for new members, and if you're *new* to town, then—"

"I am."

A glimmer of hope budded between them just then, and Betsy prayed her pressure wasn't overbearing on the girl.

"You are? Yes, well. Yes, you *are* new. And, you see, we'd just love for you to help round out our table so that when Lillian arrives, we have a good little group to distract her from her troubles. What was your name again?"

"Emily. Emily Addams."

"Emily Addams." Betsy lifted her hand, and the girl took it. They shook like a pair of newly acquainted businesswomen and shared a smile. "Welcome to Gull's Landing."

CHAPTER 6—EMILY

Emily was in no position to turn down new friends, even if they were pushy, older ones. Then again, Betsy Borden didn't look *that* old. Not even as old Emily's stepmother, who was embarrassingly young to be married to her father.

Then again, she also didn't want to make a bad impression on the waitstaff of the little café. And what if the new group wanted to tip something extravagant? Emily hardly had enough to cover her soda and salad as it was. It turned out the precious Main Street—er, rather *First* Street—eatery was no fast food joint, in price or in fare.

It also turned out that Emily's pocket change was dwindling quickly. She'd have to ask her new landlord for an extension on rent. One week into her big decision to move, and Emily was falling apart fast. Embarrassed at her lack of preparation and disappointed in her poor judgment, she figured now was not the time to turn down *any* opportunity.

Still, as Emily slid into the seat at the head of the adjacent table, she was unsure what it was she was joining exactly. A meeting of the local gardening society or a mourning session for the new widow? The one she'd see again soon, according to Mr. Grimwood.

"Funerals don't end with the burial, young lady," he'd taught her. When she'd asked when they *did* end, he simply replied, *"They don't."*

Emily didn't understand that, except for the fact that Mrs. Gulch had an outstanding bill and still hadn't decided what she'd like engraved on the headstone.

"Ladies, meet Emily Addams," Betsy declared, taking her own seat farther down the table.

Emily pressed her mouth into a thin smile as she met the gaze of each woman. She was met with narrow stares from the two younger ladies and a gaping expression from the older one, who spoke first.

"Is that your natural color?"

"*Ma!*" Betsy hissed.

Emily frowned. "My natural color?"

"No one is that blonde naturally," one of the other two added helpfully.

Emily's hand flew to her hair. "Oh. Yes. I—um—it's natural."

"It's gorgeous, hon." The older woman smiled at her then turned a sharp eye on Betsy. "You'd look great with a few highlights, Bets."

Betsy rolled her eyes playfully and winked at Emily. "Lena Borden." She lifted a hand to the woman. "AKA my *mother*." Then she moved her hand to the other two.

"Nancy and Pam. Members of the Guild who won't be around long enough for you to remember."

Emily frowned, and either Nancy or Pam gasped—Emily wasn't sure who was who.

"Well, it's true!" Betsy declared. "You won't be here for the November meeting *or* the Harvest Parade. December is out. We'll see you next year at the earliest, and who knows what'll happen by then. Maybe Lillian Gulch will unseat me as president and kick the two of you to the curb." Betsy cackled at her own joke and her mother pawed her hand at her daughter, but Emily just sat there. Awkwardly. Unsure how she might interact with these strangers who themselves seemed strange towards each other.

She stole a sip of water to busy herself.

"Emily, dear," Pam or Nancy said, her voice conspiratorial and low to match the angle of her face.

Emily choked briefly on her water, sputtering and reddening and shivering all at once.

"You okay?" Lena asked.

She nodded quickly, clearing her throat as discreetly as possible. "Yes," Emily managed. "Yes?" she looked to the woman who had addressed her. Short, mousy brown hair and beady eyes. Lots of rouge.

"Tell us, what do you *know* about what *happened* to Sam Gulch?"

Lena and the other woman leaned in.

Emily frowned.

Betsy gasped. "Oh, *please*." She looked around herself as if to ensure the five of them were alone in public. "Don't go there *again*, Nancy."

"You know what they say about rumors," added the woman Emily assumed—by her powers of deduction—to be Pam.

Lena clicked her tongue. "It's a bit over the top, *really*, Nancy."

"Well, *I* didn't start it."

Betsy waved her off. "Emily, don't listen to these nuts."

But even though Emily had been meek so far, she was a curious sort. Too curious to let such a vaguery as that pass by without just a small request for clarification. "What *happened* to him?" she emulated the woman's enunciation.

Betsy shot the others a look. "It's nothing, truly. Just small-minded, small-town gossip by the bored housewives of Gull's Landing." She winked at Emily. "You'll get used to tuning it out."

"Oh, please, Betsy," Lena huffed. "*You're* the one who started the rumor."

CHAPTER 7—LIL

Lil woke up late Sunday morning with a headache and an empty stomach. It'd be best to eat before she took another pill—the pill the doctor had prescribed her on the evening of Sam's passing.

But then, did she even need it?

Nah.

What she needed was a strong coffee. Maybe a glazed doughnut.

After a fitful several hours, she'd risen at three in the morning and sat in front of the television with a single cigarette, a glass of red wine, and a crossword. Around five, she'd slid down into the cushions of her sofa and pulled an afghan up to her chin, drifting in and out of sleep until ten, and by then, her visitors had hidden away on the back deck.

Lil had lost count of who was staying with her in the second room upstairs. Was it just her nieces and her sister-in-law?

It didn't matter. Lil didn't need the company. Really and truly, she didn't.

By eleven, Doris, Bea, and Sophia had packed their bags, albeit reluctantly.

Lil had to insist that she was meeting friends for brunch.

Ha.

What a crock.

Friends.

Still, Doris wouldn't leave unless Lil was making an exaggerated effort to get ready. And even *then*, she paused at the door.

"Lil, you could come back to Philly with the girls and me."

Lil pursed her lips. "I'm fine. Really, I'm fine, Doris."

Doris checked her watch. "You'll be late for your brunch if you don't get a move on."

"I'll hurry. I promise."

Doris didn't budge.

Lil let out a sigh. "Fine. *Fine!* I'm going." She grabbed her handbag from the front table and followed her sister-in-law out. The only way of finally and truly shaking Doris and the girls was by leaving herself.

But it wasn't like they'd follow Lil down to Maeve's. She could pretend to go there. Pretend to accept Betsy Borden's half-yoked invitation. Pretend that she needed emotional support, when in fact she *didn't*. What Lil needed was to get back to the mortuary and discuss the final details with Norman Grimwood. That's what she *needed* to do. Lay Sam and all his aftereffects to rest once and for all.

And then she recalled that the mortuary was closed on Sundays.

By sheer force of will, Lil climbed into her car and pulled out behind Doris, turning carefully in the direction of downtown Gull's Landing, if you could even call it that.

Gull's Landing was nothing like Philly, where Lil was born and raised. Now with Sam dead, she really could move home. There was nothing much tying her down to the little beachside town. Other than the fact that she could snap on her bathing suit nearly five months out of the year and fiddle with her Tarot cards and shuffle around the house like a bum. If she moved back to Philly, she'd have to put up with Doris and the others, always meddling. She'd have to wear real clothes, probably. No more swim covers in the summer or sweatsuits in the winter. City clothes.

And then there'd be the traffic to contend with. And downtown Philly was more than a downtown. It was its own city. Center City, to be specific. Did Lil really need that in her life?

Downtown Gull's Landing was a stretch of sidewalk shops and miniature restaurants that spanned First Street between Maple Avenue and Hickory Lane. It wasn't even *named* Main Street, for the love of God.

Maybe Lil sort of liked that, though.

And presently, that's precisely where Lil found herself. Parked parallel, *miraculously*, just outside of Geppetto's Dolls and Toys, one storefront down from Maeve's.

Her hands sweaty on the steering wheel, she contemplated seriously the consequences of appearing for this so-called brunch. What if it was a lowdown, dirty trick? What if Betsy Borden wanted to parade Lil out about the town like some freak show? Gull's Landing's latest widow, *look at her mourn*?

Or worse, what if they wanted to see up-close and in-person that Lil was *hardly* mourning? What if they found her out? A crook? A fraud of a wife who didn't deserve a husband or a successful marriage.

Funny that a marriage's success was tied to death like that. No, there was no divorce. They'd stuck it out until death did they part, and *poof*, black-clad widow with tears staining her cheeks—what a tragedy! What a happy couple they must have been! How madly in love! How lucky was Lil to have *that* for umpteen years? A *successful marriage.*

She scoffed and leveled her stare at the patio of the restaurant. It encroached on the sidewalk and wrapped around the corner onto Elm Street. Lil had never met Maeve, but she didn't think much of a businesswoman who flayed herself out so flamboyantly like she owned First Street.

A waving hand caught Lil's attention through the windshield.

She squinted.

There it was again, this time closer and clearly attached to a body. A broad, moving body—the body heading down the brick walk toward Lil in her car.

Betsy Borden, naturally.

"Lillian?" the voice was cloudy. Distant. Through the metal and glass of Lil's car.

She sighed and popped the door open, pushing out and offering a small smile as she pulled her sunglasses down her nose. "Betsy. Hi."

"We are *so* glad you could make it," the woman answered, rounding the hood of Lil's car and greeting her in the street, on the verge of holding up traffic. *If* there were any. Which there wasn't. Not in October. Not in Gull's Landing.

Lil had only ever met Betsy twice. The second time being at the funeral. A meeting which could have been forgettable save for Betsy's invitation for this morning.

The first time was far more awkward, somehow. Betsy and the newest set of Garden Guild ladies had been out and about on the boardwalk and had somehow made their way all the way to the far south end, to the sandy beach that spread out from Lil's backyard, where she had been sitting, reading cards for her nieces.

One of the Guild members who walked with Betsy was an acquaintance of Lil's, and she naturally struck up a conversation, introducing Betsy as the newest member of the group and effectively reminding Lil of how disinterested she was in being a joiner.

Lil was no joiner.

She was no follower.

No leader, either.

She just... *was*.

She liked the beach. She liked her Tarot cards. Her bathing suits. Her corduroy sofa and television set. She liked *Wheel of Fortune* and a good cheesecake. Red wine. The occasional cigarette—she'd quit smoking full-time years back.

Lil had a few friends scattered around the eastern seaboard. Relations. People to call and gab with. She had her nieces and their friends in the summer—a highlight in Lil's world, truly. She had church. And she'd had Sam. And all of the problems he'd created. It was enough for Lil. For years it had been enough.

She didn't need the clubs she'd joined here and there —weak efforts at ingratiating herself into her new town. Not the Beach Walkers or the BINGO Babes. Surely not that hoity-toity book club bunch. And she didn't need the Garden Guild. Even if she enjoyed the occasional house plant or pretty floral arrangement. She didn't need 'em.

"Sorry I'm late," Lil answered, dragging her handbag from the passenger seat before thrusting her door shut.

"No, no," Betsy chided. "You're not late. We just got our drinks. Do you like Arnold Palmers?"

Lil grimaced. "Um—"

"Of course you don't. You're a midday margarita gal, no doubt." Betsy grabbed Lil's free hand and threaded it through her arm, patting the back of it as she guided Lil down the sidewalk to Maeve's and a patio table where four others sat, watching.

Lil had to admit inwardly that she didn't quite mind Betsy's overbearing manner. There was comfort in it. Like a mother bear, tugging her cubs along toward a cool stream on a hot day.

She pulled them to a stop at the corner of the long patio table and pointed. "Lil, you probably know every-one, but just in case, that's Nancy. Pam. My mother, Lena. And this is Emily Addams. She's new in town and the most recent addition to the club."

Lil had stopped listening just as soon as Betsy started speaking.

Nancy. Nancy Shytle.

She had the sudden urge to bolt, but Nancy held Lil's gaze so hard that Lil knew she was challenging her to stay.

And stay, she did.

"Emily, you—you work..." Lil started, swallowing her feelings about Nancy and mustering a polite smile for the familiar blonde girl.

"For Mr. Grimwood," the girl murmured.

Lil lowered herself into the seat beside Betsy, glancing around the table as the others stared at her, murmuring hellos over the tops of their iced drinks.

"Right." Lil reached for her water, suddenly ravished by thirst.

"Emily just moved to Gull's Landing a week ago, if you can believe that."

Lil could. That was how the town worked. Just as soon as you'd unzipped your suitcase, it sank its claws right in.

"Do you live inland?" It was the most useless question Lil could have asked. Almost all locals lived inland, rather than on the beach or near the boardwalk. In fact, it was a point of embarrassment for Lil that she even lived on the beach at all. One of the reasons she shrank from the social circles. People assumed she was a Shoobie rather than a townie. Sam had never cared. He'd loved the attention. Not Lil.

"She lives with Norman Grimwood," Nancy answered icily.

Lil felt herself freeze at the woman's answer—at Norman's *name*. She forced herself to nod, but it was too late. Nancy must have seen. She must have seen that it caught Lil off guard. Because Nancy grinned like the Cheshire Cat. And Lil's blood ran cold all over again.

CHAPTER 8—BETSY

"To Sam." Betsy held her Arnold Palmer above the center of the table.

Their lunch had just arrived, and after a little small talk, Betsy felt it best to raise a glass to the man who had brought them together. Even if she didn't know him. Even if she only knew *of* him.

Lillian picked up her drink. "Sure. To Sam."

The others followed suit and, after a cascade of clicking, Betsy opted to quickly change the topic. She'd hate to pull Lillian's mood down.

"So, Lillian—"

"Lil," she answered before taking a long swig of her lemonade—Maeve's didn't serve *real* drinks until five.

"Oh. Lil. Sure, sure. So, *Lil*," Betsy went on, "I hadn't mentioned it to the girls but I'm a recent retiree, you see—"

"Retiree?" Lena Borden cut in, speaking through a mouthful of salad. "You're forty-five years old. Whatdya mean *retiree*?"

"Mother." Betsy flared her nostrils and stared the woman down. Then she blinked away the irritation and smiled at the others. "As I was saying, I've left the corporate world, you *see*—just sold our business—Book with Borden? Do you know it?" The question was for Lil and Emily, naturally.

Emily shook her head meekly. Lil just lifted an eyebrow. "Book with Borden?"

"Her father's company. A travel agency," Lena provided, again talking through a mouthful of romaine lettuce. Hopeless. Her mother was *hopeless*.

"We just sold, and it feels like—" Betsy closed her eyes and sniffed the air as she searched for the right word.

"A bologna sandwich?"

Betsy glared at Pam. "Excuse me?"

"Come on, Betsy. You paraded around the offices like a secretary." She threw a look at Emily. "No offense. But Betsy here pretends she was some executive in a boardroom and that making the choice to sell was the hardest thing she ever did."

"It was a hard decision," Betsy bemoaned. "But what I was *going* to say was that it feels like *freedom*."

"Freedom to spend all that money," Nancy huffed.

"Freedom," Emily whispered.

Betsy glanced at her. "Exactly. See?" She threw up a hand. "Emily knows what I'm talking about. *Freedom*." She eyed the pretty young blonde. What could the girl know about freedom? She was barely an adult. Twenty-five at the far outside, *maybe*. She hadn't lived long enough to be trapped in something... lost her freedom. Not yet.

Then Lillian lifted her half-full drink. "Freedom. To freedom."

Betsy shared a devilish grin with her seat neighbor— their guest of honor—before turning it on Emily. "To freedom."

"WHAT WAS *THAT* ALL ABOUT?" her mother asked once they were buckled into the Buick and back on the road heading to The Landing. The Landing was the country club community where the two shared Betsy's four-bedroom ranch-style home.

Her house sat on the ninth green, and it was the perfect spot for Betsy. From her lanai, she could spy the golfers in their pressed Dockers, their fit rears wiggling as they shifted into position for a long putt. Plus, from her property, it was a straight shot to the clubhouse for happy hour and Bingo Mondays. Betsy loved Bingo.

"What was *what* all about, Ma?" Betsy pulled into the drive and killed the engine.

"Freedom *this*! Freedom *that*! I don't get it. Women and *freedom*. What's with it?"

"Coming from the woman who told me not to give up my role in the business world or else I'd set womankind back a hundred years?" Betsy gave her mother the eye. "You're hot and cold. You know that? There's no pleasing you."

"Well, sure—I get the freedom thing with *you*. But not

with Lillian Gulch. Good Lord, Bets, she just lost her husband. *Freedom*?"

"I don't think it's our business, Ma."

Lena clicked her tongue. "It is if you're brunching with these gals. And that Emily—she had something to say about *freedom,* too."

Betsy twisted her hands around the steering wheel. Her mother had a point. And Lillian—or *Lil*, rather—did seem a little... joyous. She squeezed her eyes shut at the memory of starting that awful rumor the week before.

When the club got word of Sam's passing, the phone tree had lit up like wildfire, and somewhere along the way, Betsy had found herself whispering ideas into the leaves of the grapevine. She was stupid and cruel to do it, and she'd take it back if she could.

It just happened so fast.

Lena had been hanging around the clubhouse, and it was there that she had heard from Doctor Drier's *wife* that Sam Gulch had passed after a week-long coma. Among *other* complications. This information was all shared under the *strictest* of confidences, and Lena was not to tell a soul. So, naturally, she only told Betsy. But not to worry, she took great care to remind Betsy that the medical information was entirely privileged and it would be wholly illegal to spread such information.

Well, Betsy knew she had to alert the Garden Guild, naturally. They'd have to put together the floral arrangements, at *minimum*.

Betsy had first dialed Pam and her message was simple. Sam Gulch had passed away. That was *it*.

But then Pam had to go and ask *how* he died, and

Betsy had to preserve the medical information, so she hemmed and she hawed for a moment too long.

That's when Pam pushed. "*Betsy*," she trilled, "was it of *natural* causes?"

And again, Betsy didn't know the right answer there, so she hemmed and she hawed again, suggesting that she didn't know the details. Just that it was a private matter. A secret. Very serious. Very secret.

And that was all Betsy needed to say.

Pam called Nancy, and Nancy called the rest of the town and soon enough, there you had it: Lillian Gulch had killed her husband.

Then, at the funeral, it was all too clear that if Lillian Gulch had killed her husband, she'd gotten away with it. At least, for the time being. There were no policemen. No detectives. No interviews of the town people about what the general consensus might be.

It was just after the burial that Betsy finally huddled together with the others and, shamefully, partook in a little harmless banter.

By then, though, Betsy had come to hear a little more about good ol' Sam Gulch, and it occurred to her that if the rumors—which she *knew* to be false—even had a single iota of truth to them, well what could the harm be?

Who could really blame Lillian Gulch if she *had* killed her husband?

CHAPTER 9—EMILY

After brunch, Emily was free to explore town before settling back into her new second-floor apartment.

Having lunch with Betsy and Lillian and the others had been equal parts uncomfortable and exciting. In her life, Emily had made and lost her fair share of friends. Grade school friends got exchanged for junior high friends. Junior high friends were left behind for high school boyfriends. And by the time she graduated from the twelfth grade, Emily had no friends to her name and one lump of a first husband who was as useless as Emily's useless stepmother. The only difference was that Emily didn't have to sleep with her mean ol' stepmother.

That first marriage ended in a busted nose and a quick annulment, so technically, Emily didn't even have to count it.

She met Jimmy just weeks later. Swept her off her feet, he did. A courthouse wedding later, and Emily realized she didn't have other women to talk to. To compare marriages with. To see if her jealousies and his anger issues were normal. If what Emily had experienced so far was par for the course.

Soon enough, she came to realize that even if it *was* par for the course, she wanted no part.

Now, with a little apartment of her own, Emily knew she'd made the right choice. Even if she ended up having to take on a second job. Even if she had to suffer through expensive luncheons with Gull's Landing high society.

Betsy Borden was onto something. Freedom was worth it all.

And anyway, Mr. Grimwood wasn't so bad. He was maybe the kindest man Emily had met yet. Besides her tenth-grade geometry teacher, of course. Mr. Powers was nice *and* handsome, and that combination was too much for Emily to take. No wonder she nearly flunked out.

Emily strolled slowly down First Street, window shopping like a tourist.

Behind the broad windows of Geppetto's sat pretty dolls with hair in ringlets. They wore patterned petticoats and looked more expensive than anything Emily had ever owned in her life. Wooden horses rocked in a row in the distance beyond, and Emily thought a bit about her childhood. When had it ended? She couldn't quite figure. It felt like a very long time ago, which was no good when you were only twenty years old.

After the toy store, Emily came upon a women's clothing boutique with a French name: *Cherise*. She stood and stared at a mannequin wearing a sleek pantsuit, a thick fur stole hugging her shoulders. Was it a stole?

What *was* a stole, anyway? And could it be that a mannequin had more style than Emily?

Emily ran her hands down her slight waist and pinched the fabric of her dad's old flannel shirt. She might have put a dress on. Maybe her mint sweater, too. But she'd already worn the dress for the funeral, and the sweater had a blotchy stain across one sleeve.

The next and final shop on that stretch of storefronts was a bakery and confectionery. Goodman's Goodies. In the window, the glass bulb of a comically large gumball machine gleamed. Beside it, a window case filled with sugary candies of all varieties. Beyond the doors, a second window case and more scrumptious delights. Doughnuts and cinnamon rolls, cookies and cakes. Heaven in a glass case.

Emily made a personal promise to save up enough money every month to treat herself to something from one of the shops on First Street. One month she might order a more extravagant meal from Maeve's—something more than a dry iceberg lettuce salad. After all, Emily wasn't a salad type. She didn't need to lose weight, for one. And she didn't much care for vegetables, secondly.

After another month, maybe she could pick out her own silk scarf. Something straight off of a faceless mannequin in *Cherise*.

And then maybe after all of that she could march right into Goodman's and scoop up half a dozen of the oversized chocolate chip cookies that oozed melted chocolate.

With her plan in her head, she walked back the way she came, up toward Elm, where she'd turn right and then cut left down Second Street for another few blocks until she was past the mortuary.

Homeward bound.

To the second-floor apartment with its Chantilly lace curtains and black-and-white linoleum bathroom floor. Pedestal sink and clawfoot bathtub and creaky, sagging mattress that Emily would sink into and sleep as soundly as ever.

Freedom.

THE NEXT MORNING, Mr. Grimwood's mother—currently his only other tenant—fixed pancakes and bacon just for Emily. After, the old woman sent her down the street with a thermos of steaming coffee and a brown paper sack lunch.

Emily felt like a child all over again as she gripped the heavy sack in her hand and carefully avoided cracks in the sidewalk, humming merrily in the chilly morning air.

A full belly, a good night's sleep, and a decent job... what more could a gal want?

When she arrived at the mortuary, Mr. Grimwood was nowhere to be seen. Could be in the back seeing to newly delivered remains. Could be in his office, running numbers. He seemed to run numbers rather often. *The numbers of death*, he called them. Emily didn't understand that.

She tucked her lunch into her desk drawer and set her purse on the carpet at her feet before sliding a finger across her calendar to verify the day's schedule.

Ah yes. Lillian Gulch. Nine o'clock.

Emily's stomach churned.

It might be a little more awkward to do business with "Lil" now that they were unofficial friends and official co-members of the same club.

The thought reminded Emily to make a note in her calendar.

She flipped to the first Saturday of November.

Technically, she wasn't supposed to use the mortuary desk calendar for her own personal affairs, but she figured Mr. Grimwood wouldn't mind.

To be safe, Emily used a secret code. *G.G. MTG —B.B.'s.*

Garden Guild Meeting. Betsy Borden's house.

Emily wondered where Betsy lived and what her house would be like. She had a conflicting mental picture of the boisterous woman.

On the one hand, Betsy was comfortable and kind to strangers like Emily. She dismissed gossip and leaned toward you when she spoke to you. Big-boned with warm maple-syrup-colored hair and a broad face... it felt safe just to share the same town as Betsy.

On the other hand, she was cackling and intrusive. Her outfit was loud and expensive-looking, and her tone with her mother was sharp and unnerving to Emily, who held her elders in high regard, even when they were hardly deserving.

The front door creaked open, and Emily's attention shot up.

"Lil," she blurted, flushing before correcting herself. "Mrs. Gulch."

"Oh, please. Call me Lil, would you?"

Emily nodded earnestly. "All right. *Lil*, welcome. Good morning. Can I get you a coffee or tea? A water?"

Lil shook her head. "Let's get this over with."

She was dressed casually, in a sweatsuit. But even in the sweatsuit, she looked... *nice*. She had makeup on and her hair—a frosted blonde color—was blown stylishly back from her face, hair sprayed and set. In the crook of her elbow, her handbag. Jangling about her fingers and wrists and earlobes, jewelry. It was the same woman from the brunch and the funeral, but more approachable now. Not softer, no. But... not as *bleak*. Or black, either.

Was that how death worked? Day by day, things improved? The sheath of grief slid away and you returned to your old self in no time?

Emily suspected not. Even when her mother left— and the woman hadn't *died*... at least, not that Emily knew —Emily didn't shower for a week. She started to wonder if that was why her father brought in a new woman so soon. To set an example for his grubby, motherless child.

But maybe once you were older, things changed. Maybe it got easier to accept death as a part of life. Mr. Grimwood sure had, after all.

"I'll just let Mr. Grimwood know you're here and—"

"Lil." Her boss's soft voice materialized behind Emily. She turned and watched him move carefully toward the widow and take her hand in his.

Emily hadn't seen Mr. Grimwood interact with any bereaved other than Lil, but if this was how he treated all widows, then no wonder he was the busiest funeral director in town.

Then again, Emily wasn't entirely sure there *were* any others. Gull's Landing was small. Did it have room for a competing mortuary? Surely not every citizen of Gull's Landing would fit in the Second Street Cemetery, would they? It seemed to be nearly full. She stowed the question for later.

"Emily, will you join us in my office? We'll just go over the final paperwork."

"Yes, sir," Emily answered, following the two into his wood-paneled room in the center of the building.

Green plants stood in each corner and a vase of cheery flowers sat on the edge of the desk. One of Emily's jobs was to water every plant in the entire mortuary, and she loved doing it. It relaxed her. She made a mental note to change the water in the vase after Lil had gone.

Later, she'd take to the grounds to inspect every last headstone. Mr. Grimwood liked doing that himself, he said, but it would be a good way to train Emily up.

Look for dead flowers, weeds, trash—anything offensive, he'd taught her.

The groundskeeper handled raking leaves and trimming hedges. Humidity and rain handled the grass. As for the flowers and bushes that grew in the tree wells and along the back gate, Emily offered to keep a close eye, telling Mr. Grimwood that she had a little experience with foliage. He'd liked that and allowed her to do just that—become the third-in-command gardener, of sorts. Behind himself and the groundskeeper, that was. Anyway, the little chore gave her a chance to sneak outside for fresh air and sunshine in the middle of the day. Working in a funeral home, it was important to take a break among living things. Even if the living things happened to grow over dead things.

"The engraving, Lil," Mr. Grimwood started, his hands in a neat pile on top of his desk. "Have you made any decisions there?"

Lil flashed a glance at Emily, who offered a small smile in return, her notebook and pencil poised on her lap.

"What's standard?" Lil asked. "I think I'll go with whatever is standard."

"Well," Mr. Grimwood tugged a binder out from a nearby shelf. "I have several examples we can take a look at. Maybe you'll find something in here." He opened the black cover and swiveled the thing toward Lil and Emily. Each laminated page offered photographs of local headstones and, beneath them, transcriptions of the epitaphs.

He flipped back to the first page, which showed two older headstones.

Lil pressed her finger on the first photograph, her long red nail tapping softly on the plastic. "This looks good."

Emily glanced at Mr. Grimwood, who cleared his throat.

"Just his name and the dates, then?" Mr. Grimwood blinked.

"It's a small marker," Lil responded. "We don't have room for much more."

"Lil." He lowered his voice. "I know this isn't my business but—"

Emily shifted uncomfortably in her chair, her focus

on the blank white page where she was set to document Lil's wish for Sam's epitaph.

"Go on, Norman," Lil replied. "My business isn't my own. Not in this town." Though the words were harsh, her tone was light, and it occurred to Emily that she was joking with Norman. An inside joke, perhaps?

But he didn't laugh or smile. He laced his fingers on the desk. "Lil, it's no secret that Sam left you in good condition."

"Psh," Lil breathed. "That's all relative, now, isn't it?"

Emily felt her throat constrict. Whatever they were talking about... it was *not* Emily's business. Even if it *was* the town's business or whatever Lil meant.

Then, out of the clear blue, a sob escaped from somewhere deep inside of Lil. A hollow, shaking sob.

Frightened, Emily couldn't help but recoil.

Mr. Grimwood stood and grabbed a box of tissues, rounding his desk. "Miss Addams, will you excuse us?"

Emily's stomach clenched harder. "Of—of course." She shot up, nearly dropping her notebook and pencil. "I'll just... I'll just be at my desk. If you need me."

Without another word, she slipped out the door and closed it behind her, breathing hard. If she'd been better at her job, she'd have patted Lil on the shoulder. She'd have murmured something more helpful. Meaningful. Useful.

But that was the problem with Emily. She was probably just as useless as the people who'd raised her.

Unwilling to settle for such a truth, she perched on the edge of her chair and tapped her pencil neurotically on her desk calendar, thinking hard about something she could do to *help* for once. Instead of running. Instead of crying. Instead of blaming the world for her troubles or falling victim to them.

Nothing immediately came to mind, so she looked around the lobby, searching for an answer.

Her eyes landed on the coffee table in the waiting area. On top of it, a neat display of magazines. Yesterday's paper. A Bible. A phonebook.

An idea struck her. Maybe she could call Betsy. Betsy Borden. Betsy would know what to do. She could help. Maybe she could plan another brunch. Maybe that's what grown women did for each other. They set up brunches, and Lil needed another one. Another escape from her pain and sorrow.

She stood and strode to the table and hefted up the phonebook, returning to her desk before settling it on top of her calendar. First, Emily thumbed to the residential pages.

Lena Borden's name was there, plain as day, but no phone number was listed. Her husband's name was not there, and Emily wondered if he'd passed, too.

There was no Betsy Borden but there was a Lizbeth Borden. Her number was also unlisted.

Emily sighed and thrummed her fingers again on the desk.

She had another idea.

Fanning quickly to the business pages, she found Book with Borden right away. A full-page advertisement, complete with an image of an airplane soaring across the thin yellow sheet.

Emily glanced at Mr. Grimwood's office door. She felt

for poor ol' Lil. Really she did. And to see the hint of a smile... a bit of joy that had come out during the brunch... Emily knew she was about to make the right call.

She punched the number into her phone and was directed immediately to a cheery secretary.

"Book with Borden today and get ten percent off your booking fee. This is Celeste, where are we traveling to today?"

Emily stifled a giggle. She imagined herself using a similar sort of tagline when people called the funeral home. *Second Street Mortuary, who are we burying today?*

CHAPTER 10—LIL

It felt good to cry. To cry *hard*.

As Norman handed her tissue after tissue and sat beside her, patting her shoulder and keeping as silent as a mouse, Lil wondered what life might have been like had she had someone like that at home with her all those years—all the hard years. During the move and then after. When she'd lost her brother to cancer. When she'd crossed the threshold of forty and made her way to fifty and her body changed and solidified the truth that she'd always be just an aunt. Where was the soft pat? The quiet listening?

After another moment, she composed herself and swallowed down the last of the tears. "Thanks, Norman," she murmured, dabbing beneath her eyes with a tissue. A final shudder vibrated her lips.

"That's what I'm here for. Now, Lil, are you *sure*?"

"About the engraving?" she asked, her gaze settling again on the simple headstone in the black-and-white snapshot.

"Yes. Just his name and the dates?"

Lil nodded with finality. "Absolutely. It's more than enough, really."

"What about you?" Norman asked, his pen hovering above a leather-bound notepad.

"Me?" Lil frowned. "What about me?"

"Usually, Lil, when one spouse dies, the other takes the opportunity to arrange a family plot."

"*Family?*" The word stung her tongue like poison.

When Lil thought of family she thought of Bea and Sophia and Di. Hell, she thought of *Doris*, even. Not Sam, though.

"A marital plot, if you'd prefer?" Norman tried.

Lil blinked. "I understand."

Silence filled the air between them as she sucked in a breath.

"You can hold off." Norman gently closed the binder on the desk then his notepad, his long fingers pressing into the supple leather. "I'll send the engraving off. You call me if you need anything." Lil nodded, but Norman laid a hand on her shoulder again. "Anything, Lil. Do you hear me?"

"Yes." She met his gaze. "Thank you, Norman."

Rising, she collected her bag and sniffled one last time, wondering what happened next. "How long does it take?"

"Pardon?"

She cleared her throat. "The engraving. Will I need to come back?"

"You mean, *when* it's done—will you come back to... *see* it?"

"Right." Lil replied with a short nod.

"Well, that's up to you. Usually, people do."

"Of course." Lil nodded again, thinking hard. A pause, and then, "You have my number?"

Norman smiled. "Of course."

AFTER LIL LEFT Norman's office, she caught sight of the secretary, who was on the phone. She gestured to Lil and whispered "Hi," one hand on the mouthpiece, her manner awkward.

Emily was young, Lil knew. Plain as day, the girl was young and *new* to the job. She'd get hold of things. Lil saw something in Emily, though. A spark that she had once had. Lord, maybe Lil *still* had it. Buried somewhere deep down. She pursed her lips and wondered if she ought to pass her phone number on to Emily, too. It wouldn't be until November that they'd see each other again—for the Garden Guild monthly meeting. Assuming the engraving took as long as Norman had implied. And assuming Lil decided to actually show up at the ol' club crap.

Just as she was about to move toward the door, uncommitted to the idea of sharing her phone number with a veritable teenager, Emily held a hand up. "Won't you wait just a moment, Lil?"

The girl's quick adoption of Lil's nickname made her smirk. She nodded and crossed her arms over her chest.

"All right, then," Emily said into the receiver. "Yes, that'll do... Right... Tonight at six... Mhm... The country club, yes... No, no. I'm sure I'll find it. Okay, *Borden*, yes... I'll mention it, all right... Mhmm... Yes, goodbye, now— oh! And *thank you*." The girl cradled the phone back on its base and blew a puff of air that lifted her blonde wisps. "Whew!"

Lil lifted one eyebrow, expectant.

"Thank you so much for waiting, Mrs. Gulch—I mean *Lil*. I took the liberty of placing a phone call just as the two of you were finishing up, you see." Emily's eyes darted left and Lil looked back. Norman had joined them. Butterflies rippled up Lil's stomach, and she tried hard to squash them. How *indecent*, truly.

"A phone call?" She tried to focus and directed the girl back to her point.

"Right, yes," Emily replied. "I, um... well, now that we are in the Garden Guild together, of course, you see, I figured—"

"Emily," Norman sang out her name as a partial reprimand.

She paled, but Lil shot him a look. "Go ahead, Emily." She smiled kindly.

"Right, well. Mrs. Gulch—*Lil*, I was wondering if you might like to join the Garden Guild for Bingo night?"

DESPITE IT BEING the end of October, the weather was warm enough that Lil preferred to sit outside for the rest of the day. Particularly if she was going to be cooped up in some stuffy country club restaurant with a slew of

Polo-wearing snobs while some hack called out Bingo numbers.

Upon her return home, she felt the cloud of absence. Sam's absence. Despite it all, it was odd for him to be... just... gone. And for Lil to be... just... alone.

She studied the contents of the fridge for a minute too long, settling at last on a slice of cheesecake and a glass of milk, which she carried to the backyard.

Brisk ocean air whipped across her face, and Lil welcomed the humidity. It'd give her cotton-candy bob a little boost before the night. A little body.

Though she had no real excuse, Lil's backyard had grown over with weeds. Sand crept in across the grass, dulling its green. Sand blanketed the steps up to the back stoop. Sand had worn away the white paint on the little picket fence.

Sand, sand, sand.

It wasn't just sand and weeds that were the problem, though.

Dead flowers withered in the planters that stood on either side of the doorway. In fact, they were probably the worst offenders. At least the sand was inevitable. Not dead flowers, though. Those, she ought to have handled by now.

Lil clicked her tongue before sliding a forkful of cheesecake between her lips.

Her eyes danced to the far side of the yard, where she used to keep a vegetable garden, back when she was young and full of the stuff young women are typically full of. Dreams and hopes for a happy home and a pretty little garden, for example.

It used to be that Lil followed the Farmer's Almanac. She'd lay down beets and carrots, onions and turnips in early October. Roots came a little later. Cleaning out the beds and planting a few late-season mums after the veggies. Lastly, bulbs for the next spring. But prep work for food and herbs came first. That's how it was for Lil, the product of the Great Depression.

As she took a second bite, something caught her attention: a green rope snaking across the garden bed and trailing off between two slats of the fencing and out into the beyond, south of the property.

She set the cheesecake down and strode over, curious at the intruder. Or was it?

Nearing the old bed, she saw that there was more to the plant than just green stem and full leaves. It was a full-blown vine, its tendrils all crawling out of the backyard as if to escape.

Lil mounted the low wall of the bed and braced herself against the fence before peering over it and spotting there, in a sunny patch of beach, a pumpkin, of all things.

Bewildered at the little surprise, Lil rushed to the gate and rounded over to the far side yard, an area she hadn't explored in ages—if ever.

There it was, sitting in all its bumpy, round, orange glory: a small, single pumpkin. Growing in Lil's own defunct garden on the Jersey shore.

She racked her brain for where the seed could have come from. It had been years and years since Lil had tried to grow any vegetables, let alone pumpkins. Then she recalled. The girls. The year before, the girls had visited a week before Halloween. They had carved pumpkins in the backyard and stayed up all night in front of the television, stacks of scary movie tapes looming in the corner.

Maybe a little life had found its way there, to Lil's own dreary, weedy slice of the shore. Maybe there was more to be found, too.

Discovering the little autumn charm, Lil whipped back into the yard and stood at the gate, hands on hips, examining the space. She thought hard about the season and about the tools in the little shed on the side of the house. She thought about the fact that she had all the time in the world. She didn't have anyone there to pester her. She didn't have anyone around to read cards for. Wheel of Fortune wasn't on for hours and anyway—Bingo night with the girls.

The girls. Lil let out a short laugh.

And then, she went to the shed. Because if Lil was going to Bingo night with the Garden Guild—if she was officially rejoining their ranks—well, then, she'd better have a garden to speak of.

CHAPTER 11—BETSY

The last time Betsy had courted new company to Bingo night was on a date gone wrong. Some slick-talking casino manager with a penchant for numbers. The sad part was just how good he had smelled. Betsy liked when a man smelled good. But things fell apart after the first round of the game went to a younger guy on the next table over. Not even a second drink—or a third, for that matter—was enough to save Betsy's date from his ridiculous jealousies. Funny, though, because Betsy could appreciate the passion. She, herself, took Bingo too seriously. Maybe therein laid the rub. It wouldn't do to have competition... or someone equally competitive. Not for Betsy Borden.

Ever since then, she had preferred to keep it to just her mother, as far as a Bingo date went.

This allowed Betsy to focus. She typically worked two cards, one sherry and a bowl of popcorn, and even that was more than she could handle at times. Throw in someone to entertain, and it could be a night-spoiler all over again.

And yet when sweet, meek, little Emily Addams rang Betsy up—she claimed to get the house number from the company—there was no turning the poor thing down. Betsy suspected it took either a lot of confidence or a traumatic event to put the call through. She was right on both accounts, because when Emily explained herself, it came out that Lil was having a harder time with the whole Sam thing than any one of them had realized.

At least, according to the new girl. Betsy wasn't sure whether Emily had a keen sense about human nature, though. It could very well be a false alarm. An act. But then, wasn't this her chance to make good on starting that horrid rumor?

Maybe.

Betsy thought carefully about whether to drag Pam and Nancy into the whole mess, too, but quickly decided against it. It was one thing to add two newbies to Bingo night. It was a whole other thing to ruin the evening.

She pulled together a good Bingo outfit—red linen pants with a white button-down and a black silk scarf.

"Ma!" she called as she grabbed her purse and keys from the kitchen bar. "You ready?"

Lena descended the staircase in a nylon sweatsuit and white sneakers.

"What in the—" Betsy shook her head. "Ma, you're not going to the club in a sweatsuit and sneakers. Go change."

"I did change. Out of that God-awful pair of black slacks that pinched my stomach skin. This is it. This is what I'm wearing, Betsy. And besides, have you seen some of those old ladies who show up? They practically wear pajamas. I look good compared to half of them."

"You got that pretty new wrap from *Cherise* yesterday. Put it on. Besides, what if you see Greg?"

Lena gave Betsy a look. "I don't care what Greg Rosen sees me in! There's nothing there, Betsy. I've told you. Nothing!"

Greg Rosen lived three streets over and also happened to attend Bingo religiously. He had an obvious thing for Lena, but Lena swore up and down that she didn't return his interest.

Lena Borden was that way—easy to hear and hard to read. A true contradiction of humanity. Or, perhaps, a good example of the dual nature of women.

Once, years after John had passed, Lena came down sick with a bad bout of bronchitis. She was in the hospital for less than a day, but it was enough time for her to get a saline drip. Once duly hooked up, she whispered for Betsy to join her at her bedside where she attempted, through several episodes of sputtering and coughing, to tell Betsy that she had to tell her something.

Then, the nurse came in, outfitted in bright white hospital scrubs with rubber-soled clogs. "You're free to go, Mrs. Borden!" the kindly medical woman had chirped merrily, and after that, Betsy never heard another word about the deathbed secret that almost was.

Even when she asked her mother days later, "What was it you were going to tell me?" Lena had waved her off.

"Oh, nothing. Nothing."

But "nothing" with Lena Borden was always "something."

Which was exactly why Betsy knew there was more going on with ol' Greg Rosen. Particularly when Lena arrived by her side at the front door and Betsy detected an extra coat of mascara on the woman's short lashes.

"THERE THEY ARE," Lena hissed, nodding her head in the general direction of the entrance.

Betsy squinted across the room to the wooden doors. "Who?" she replied.

"Greg and Bill," Lena answered.

"Ma, I thought you meant the girls." Sure enough, when Betsy looked just left of the doors, toward the bar, there were two men, their hands in their pockets as they chatted affably with the bartender. "Who's the younger one?"

"He's a new club member," Lena answered, her voice too loud. "Greg's neighbor. They play tennis together on Saturdays. He works for Pelican Pier. Management something or other."

Betsy eyed her mother. "And how do you know all this?"

"I'm on the HOA board, you forget."

"Ma, you are not on the board."

"I go to the meetings," Lena sang back.

"And they've had to kick you out, too." Betsy shook her head. "I'm going up to get our drinks and popcorn. Unless you want to?"

"No, no. You go." As Lena answered, her eyes narrowed on the gentlemen.

Betsy paused. "Maybe you should go, Ma. It seems like Greg is looking for you, anyway."

"He can look all night, if he wants. I'll stay here and save our seats. Keep my eye on the door."

Betsy smirked and shook her head before heading up to the bar.

She kept to the far end, disinterested in entangling herself in her mother's affairs, but as soon as she asked for two sherries, Greg shuffled along down the waxy wooden bar—right toward her.

Willing the bartender to work faster, Betsy scanned the room for a different familiar someone—anyone to greet. But the truth was, she and Lena had arrived half an hour early, and she had only told Lil and Emily to show up at ten 'til the hour.

"Lena's girl, am I right?" the white-haired man asked. For his age, Greg looked good. Betsy had to give him that.

"Yes." She nodded and smiled, thrumming her finger-tips on the bartop.

"Bill, have you met Betsy? Another neighbor," Greg gestured to Betsy.

The second gentleman stepped forward, and Betsy gave him a good look. Tall, lean, and dweebish. Poindexter with a pocket protector. Coke-bottle glasses. A clean-shaven face and a thick head of dark hair, graying at the temples.

"Betsy Borden of Shearwater Street." She stuck out her hand. "Welcome to The Landing."

CHAPTER 12—EMILY

Emily missed the bus. Maybe it was intentional. Not because she didn't want to go to Bingo night with her new club—and friends—but because who wanted to show up to a country club in a city bus? Or town bus, as the case may be.

In all likelihood, they wouldn't even let her in, if that was the case.

She'd envisioned arriving at the gate, manned by a security guard, and stepping down in her frumpy jeans and t-shirt, a veritable runaway. The bus doors would *woosh* closed. The heaving beast of a transportation vehicle would back out just as Emily gave her name to the round-bellied man who held the keys to the kingdom. Maybe he'd call the police.

With such an image in mind, she had taken extra care to wash and dry her hair and had selected the best dress she owned—a black sweater-knit thing that was itchy and hot and generally miserable. By the time she'd smeared on a glob of pink lipstick, she had checked the clock to see that she'd missed the bus.

By then, she figured she'd made a grave mistake. After all, with no way to get to the country club, she was no better off than if she'd arrived and been kicked off of the property.

Still, Emily skipped down the staircase in the Grimwood home, easing into a seat at the kitchen table.

Norman Grimwood's mother turned from drying her last dish and coughed into her fist. "Are you going out tonight, dear?" She lifted a suspicious eyebrow and Emily felt all the worse. What did the woman think? That one week into her new town and Emily was already on the prowl for a date?

She came clean immediately. "Betsy Borden invited me to play Bingo at her club tonight, but I've missed the bus." Emily hated to sound like a charity case, but what choice did she have?

She *was* a charity case. Just not one who was seeking any more charity than she'd already earned. She'd had all the opportunities at that that she'd needed. Now was the time to *do* something with the charity. Which was why she was trying to get to the country club in the first place.

The woman coughed again and pushed her knobby-knuckled fist into her chest, wincing. She didn't seem well. "You were going to take the public bus to The Landing?"

Emily shrugged uselessly but frowned at the woman. "Are you okay, Mrs. Grimwood? Can I get you a glass of water?"

"Norman!" The woman wailed through the thin walls of the old Victorian house, her voice rattling and a fresh fit of coughing bringing her to a seat at the small kitchen table.

Cringing, Emily shook her head. "No, no. I can walk. Really, Mrs. Grimwood." She crossed to the sink and ran water into a glass, passing it over.

But even the gesture didn't change the woman's mind or actions. "Norman, come here!" She coughed again then took a long swig of the water, her hand trembling on the glass.

Mr. Grimwood arrived in the doorway to the kitchen, more casual-looking than usual in worn jeans and a white t-shirt. Younger looking, too. He pulled reading glasses from his nose and folded them into one hand. The other hand held a rolled-up newspaper and a pen. So, he was a crossword puzzle type of man. Figured.

"Norman, Betsy Borden invited Emily to attend Bingo night at The Landing. Problem is, Norman, she has no way to get there." The slight woman leaned toward her son, her white hair on the fritz atop her head and her frail body creaking audibly as she shifted in the wooden chair.

"I'll drive you," Mr. Grimwood replied simply, with a smile. "Let me just grab my sweater."

Emily thanked Mrs. Grimwood and rose from the table. She'd offer to pay him. Or to pick up extra chores around the house. Something as a way to prove that she wasn't a burden. Nothing would be worse than to start down the same path that had led her to Gull's Landing, after all. Being a burden on others.

Within ten minutes, they were driving down Second Street and turning toward the stretch of road that cut through the center of town—First Street, naturally.

Emily loved how simple a town it was. A little grid on which she could find her way just about anywhere. Unless it was late and dark, in which case, she wouldn't dare.

"Mr. Grimwood, I'll do more around the house. I can wash and hang laundry. Yard work, too."

He looked at her from the corner of his eye. "Oh? Well... thank you, Emily. But why?"

"For driving me tonight. I won't make a habit of needing a ride around town, I promise. It's just that this club meeting was last minute, and then when I thought about the bus and the destination—well... by then I wasn't ready and it was too late and—"

"It won't do to arrive at The Landing in a public bus, that's true," he answered. "But we don't need more help around the house. You do plenty, Emily."

Not the sort to accept that, Emily pushed back. "I can rake the leaves. It's almost time to rake for the season. I can rake."

"I like to rake the leaves," Mr. Grimwood replied thoughtfully.

"Or maybe something at the mortuary?" she tried.

He gave her another sidelong look. "Emily, my giving you a ride is no big deal. Really. I needed a break anyway."

"From your crossword?" she blurted out.

A heavy sigh escaped his lips. "That," he answered lifelessly. "And the news."

Emily frowned. She was no follower of news. Mr. Grimwood could be referencing something political. Or a natural disaster. Whatever he needed a break from, she had no clue what it was and had only two options for a response. Pretend like she *did* know all about the news and nod along. Or, well, *ask*.

Sincere to a fault, Emily replied, "What happened in the news?"

He turned left up a dimly lit, private road. "Oh, well —" Mr. Grimwood eyed her again. "Nancy Shytle and her husband, Roy—there's talk they'll open a second cemetery. Something about expanding Gull's Landing and needing to consider what to do with the fine citizens who wish to be buried among family. They think Second Street doesn't have the capacity." He snorted. "Nancy Shytle is full of it. Doesn't know what she's talking about."

"Nancy Shytle?" Emily echoed. "Is that the same Nancy as the one in the Garden Guild?"

"The Garden Guild?" Mr. Grimwood raised his eyebrow.

"The gardening club—the one I'm meeting tonight. With Mrs. Borden and Mrs. Gulch?"

"Oh, right. Right. Um—" he frowned. "I suppose so. Mousy-haired gal?"

Emily stifled a smile at his description. Mr. Grimwood was no good at concealing his observations. "I've only met her once. At brunch yesterday, actually. But, yes. I'd say she has hair the color of a mouse, yes."

Mr. Grimwood's mouth twitched into a smile as they pulled to a stop in front of a round-bellied security guard, just as Emily had envisioned.

"Name and host?" the cranky man growled.

Mr. Grimwood relaxed his hands on the steering wheel. "Miss Emily Addams for Miss Betsy Borden. Bingo night."

"In the clubhouse. Take the roundabout." The man stepped back and, like magic, the gate opened.

Emily wondered what it would be like to live behind a guarded iron gate. Sure, it seemed, well, *safe*. But who were these country club folks keeping out?

What were they keeping *in*?

CHAPTER 13—LIL

Lil didn't mind a little Bingo. She'd been to the Tuesday games at St. Gertrude's a few times over the years. Normally with Sam, who enjoyed gambling, naturally. Still, the memory of sharing a card with him wasn't enough to keep Lil from her first night out as a widow.

Nothing would keep her from that. Even a trip to the hoity-toity country club on the north side of town.

Planters full of greenery decorated the front patio of the clubhouse. Lil spotted ornamental cabbage and pansies. Some Black-eyed Susans, too. A pretty display that may not last through frost. Then again, at a place like The Landing, anything was possible. Even winter blooms. They probably stowed the flowers in a green-house through to spring. Something Lil ought to invest in.

Maybe she could ask Betsy about it. That was the point of their get-together, after all.

Lil tugged her white sweater down below her waist,

feeling nervous in her polyester trousers and simple blouse. What did people wear to Bingo night in a country club?

She was about to find out.

"Lillian!" a voice called out just as she stepped through the tiled lobby and onto the soft carpet of the clubhouse dining room. Lil scanned the space until her gaze landed on Betsy, who waved wildly from a table near the host.

A little embarrassed, Lil quickly made her way to Betsy and found that she was the last to arrive.

"So glad you could make it, Lil," Emily said softly, smiling as she lifted a glass of pink lemonade to her lips.

Lil smiled back. "Yeah. Me, too." Then she nodded at Lena who passed Lil a thick Bingo card. "Thanks, Mrs. Borden."

"My mother-in-law was Mrs. Borden." The old woman cackled to herself, apparently pleased at the joke.

"Ma," Betsy groaned.

"Call me Lena," the woman added, shooing Betsy off and taking a long swig of an amber drink.

"Here's yours. Sherry. Hope you drink sherry?" Betsy passed Lil a glass then held her own up. "To the first official meeting of the new and improved Garden Guild," she said.

"New and improved?" Lil asked, clinking glasses with the others before they returned their drinks to their mouths greedily.

"I figure now that we have two new members, we might as well be new and improved. Besides, I'll need a refresher. We haven't met as an actual *gardening* club

since July. I can't even tell what kind of flowers these are."
Betsy pointed to a crystal vase full of mums.

"Mums. How can you not know what mums are?"
Lena rolled her eyes. "Have I failed you as a mother?"

"Chrysanthemums," Emily added seriously.

"*Mums.*" Lil winked at Betsy and took a sip of her
drink, wincing at its strength. They didn't mess around at
the country club.

"Sounds like you were a smart recruit," Betsy tipped
her glass to Emily. "You know your flowers."

"I worked for a florist for a little while," Emily
answered proudly. "I like to keep up with that sort of
thing, though."

"What's your favorite flower?" Betsy asked.

Lena added, "Or *plant*. Nothing wrong with a good
plant. I mean, if we care a thing about gardening, then we
know there's more to it than perennial blooms."

"Daisies," Emily answered without hesitation. "Or
lilacs."

"Beautiful. Mine are roses," Betsy replied. "Ma's are—
what? Daffodils?"

"You know me well, buttercup." Lena drew a handful
of popcorn. "I admire plants, though. You know? A good,
hardy plant. Like a potato or a peanut plant. But when it
comes right down to it, daffodils have my heart."

The others laughed.

"How about you, Lillian? Oh—sorry. Lil." Betsy held
her hand to her oh-shaped mouth, her eyes widening
playfully.

Lil considered the question. "I have lots. Orchids.
Lilies, naturally." She let a wry smile creep across her

mouth. "I love a pretty zinnia. But I have to agree with Lena. There's something about vegetable plants or herbs, even. Here's a funny story about plants and gardening," she went on, finding herself recounting how she discovered the sneaky little pumpkin plant climbing through her fence, trying to escape her yard.

"Sounds like Sheba," Betsy answered.

"Sheba?" Lil lifted an eyebrow.

"My cat. She's known for running away. Night or day, we can't keep her in place. Just about drives me nuts, I tell you what. How about you, Emily? Got any pets?"

Lil studied Betsy. She was masterful at it—the human connection thing. Moving easily between topics. Enjoying her sherry and her popcorn in equal measure and smiling and laughing at the right moments.

Emily shook her head. "I didn't bring any. I don't think Mr. Grimwood would like that anyway. He's particular."

"Good ol' Norm." Betsy tossed a handful of popcorn into her mouth.

Lil looked at her again, this time more curiously. "Do you know Norman well? Norman Grimwood?"

Betsy shook her head. "Nope. Different circles. That's assuming he has a circle."

"That's assuming *you* have a circle," Lena pointed out to her daughter.

But Betsy had become immediately distracted. Her attention focused on the man at the microphone just feet away. "Shh," she hissed. "Game's about to start."

Lena gave Lil and Emily an eyeroll, but she lifted her

card to her eyes, adjusted her glasses, and rubbed her hands together, settling deeper into her seat.

The next thirty-minutes carried on with limited chatter. Absent was any talk of garden business. Any talk of anything, in fact, as Betsy bemoaned each letter-number combination that wasn't a match for her card.

Finally, after the first round had ended and Betsy—along with the rest of them—had *lost*, she threw her arms up. "I'm getting two cards next round." Then she pointed a critical finger at her mother. "I told you not to mess with my *process*, Ma."

"Oh, please. You don't win no matter what you do." Lena hooked a thumb to the table behind them. "Twenty bucks says Greg Rosen won five calls ago and didn't even realize it."

"Who's Greg Rosen?" Lil asked, the name ringing a bell. That's how it was in small towns. Names rang bells. That was about it, though. At least for someone who stuck to the fringe of society. Someone like Lil.

"Ma's sweetheart." Betsy raised her eyebrows at Emily and Lil.

The older woman sniffed angrily. "He's not my *sweetheart*."

"But he wants to be," Betsy replied.

As if on cue, a man's voice, aged and high-pitched, came in behind them. "Well, hello!"

"Oh, here we go." Betsy smirked at Lil who glanced up at the older gentleman.

White-haired and slightly crooked from the waist up, he was neat and clean and... *charming*. Lil wondered what he'd done for a living. He looked terribly opposite of Sam

—whose weathered, leathery skin and crinkled eyes had aged him. This Greg gentleman, though clearly elderly, still made for a dashing figure. It was no wonder there was a glimmer of something between him and the indomitable Lena Borden, white-haired and fierce herself.

Lena took a swig of her sherry, downing the last of it then studying the empty chamber.

"Greg, this is Lil and Emily. Lil and Emily, meet Greg. A *neighbor*." Betsy emphasized the word "neighbor" for some reason unclear to Lil.

"Ladies," Greg answered, whistling faintly through his teeth, "Nice to meet you."

"Where's your friend, Greg?" Lena asked.

Betsy shook her head dramatically. "No, no. The second game is about to start. We don't have time for more introductions."

Still, despite Betsy's objections, Lil could have sworn she saw the woman's eye linger on the handsome stranger who walked up and joined Greg.

Lil suppressed a grin, but it fell away naturally as Norman Grimwood came to mind. Seeing the two men try their hand at flirting made her think about the kindly funeral director. Just out of reach. Never quite out of her head, though.

"I'm going to grab cards and a second round. More popcorn, girls?" Betsy asked.

"I can grab it for you," the unnamed man offered. "I can appreciate the whole *Bingo* thing. Your dedication to the game." He lowered his voice. "Except for me it's Backgammon."

Lil had expected him to say poker. It's what Sam would have said, after all. It struck her that not all men were like Sam.

Take Norman, for example.

After a brief beat, Betsy waved the man on. "Sure. Yeah. Um—two sherries, a lemonade, and a bowl of popcorn, please. I'll grab the cards. You in?" She dipped her chin to him.

"Oh, no. We have our own seats." He gestured back and Lil caught the older man—Greg—grimace.

"Suit yourselves. Two cards for me. One for each of my girls," Betsy said. "Bill, right?"

He nodded.

"Thanks," she added, and this time, Lil was *positive* Betsy gave him the eye.

CHAPTER 14—LIL

After almost a week of working in the yard and wondering what in the world she was supposed to do, Lil set up her Tarot cards on the back deck and tugged her space heater out there on an extension cord. The air was growing chillier by the day, and soon she'd stow the cards for the winter, taking them back out again once spring hit and tourists trickled back to the boardwalk.

Lil didn't read cards for money... or even for truth. She read for fun. For the most part, at least. It all started back when she and Sam had first moved to Gull's Landing.

She had picked it up like a habit after a particularly rousing reading she had purchased herself from a Gypsy on the boardwalk. Some hairy-chinned woman with long pinky nails and sharp teeth. The woman had pulled—and Lil would never forget this—a Three of Swords. It should have been a bad omen.

But Lil had thought it was a good one.

"Separation," the gnarled woman had purred. "A broken heart, no?" She had tapped with her stubby forefinger on the image of three swords piercing at odd angles through a heart.

Lil shook the memory.

It was Sunday and, at the very heart of autumn, she knew there may not be much traffic on the beach. Even so, at least until true bitter cold arrived, she could count on the odd beach walker—maybe a man with his dog or a mother with her fussy toddler—to stomp through the sand and pass the beach house, and Lil could pull the cards and think about who that stranger was. What was in store for him. Or her.

In fact, no one of any interest to Lil ended up strolling past that morning, and she decided against the cards after all, instead savoring her mug of coffee and the fleeting stream of hot air at her feet as she stared at her little garden. The pumpkin plant was now harvested— the lone pumpkin itself sat in the center of her kitchen table. Hay covered the shorn stems of other various plants and bushes, protecting against frost.

After she finished her coffee, Lil dragged the heater back inside and got ready for Mass before folding herself into her car and heading out.

As Lil drove into town and west onto Finch Street, where St. Gertrude's sat in all its ancient glory, Lil considered the contradiction of her Tarot cards and her Catholic faith. It wasn't *really* a contradiction, since the cards were for sport more than anything.

Still, what would the priest think? Lil thought about what the cards had meant to her all those years and how they'd given her some version of reprieve in the face of living with Sam Gulch for so, so long.

Maybe she didn't need the distraction anymore. Maybe she was done with Tarot. Done with pining for good news. A better future.

When she arrived at the church, she found the main parking lot to be overflowing. Sighing, Lil veered around and cut up, further west and deeper into the recesses of the parish property.

Beside the rectory, two parking spots sat empty. Lil parked in one and hopped out of her car, glancing at her watch to see that she was ten minutes late.

Ten whole minutes.

It'd be a crime to enter Mass so late. It would set Lil's nerves on fire to draw attention to the back of the parish hall. Father Bart may even say something. Something innocent or something derisive, Lil never could be sure with this particular priest. He was sarcastic to a fault and boisterous besides.

Too uncomfortable to be late, she thought of a plan. Lil could pass the time and join the eleven o'clock Mass. She'd be early, even. And what with a light chill in the air it'd do Lil good to take a long walk around the area. Warm her up before sitting in a cold wooden pew for an hour.

Anyway, the church property was sprawling and beautiful. The best part of the inland side of town.

On the west side of Gull's Landing—where Second Street gave way to Finch Street—beachfront properties gave way to residential homes and then to a thickly wooded forest. And then, beyond that, stretched the New

Jersey countryside. Cranberry bogs and wide-open space. The best part of town during the colder months. You could tuck yourself away among the trees and shrubs and underbrush. Or you could spread out in a scar of grassy farmland and feel nearly as warm and comforted as if you were snuggled beneath an afghan. At least, Lil thought so. She didn't mind taking long lonesome walks. It'd become one of those breaks—those escapes—she'd carved out for herself in what was quickly becoming "the Sam years."

Just weeks out from her husband's death, it was funny how distant she felt from him now.

She picked her way past the rectory and down a narrow trail hidden along a gentle hillside.

At the base, a shallow, weedy clearing spread out.

Lil shrugged her purse higher up on her shoulder and made her way through the bramble, wondering where the seemingly secret path may take her when her foot caught on a thick, hidden stone. She sailed forward, falling on the heels of her hands into a moist blanket of leaves.

She righted herself, pushing up with the aid of the chunky stone and examining her outfit for signs of wear. A fresh run bled up the shin of her panty hose. Bits of muck stuck to her knees, and she wiped them off as best she could. Her lower back throbbed dully—the effect of her reaction to falling and her attempt to *not* fall, no doubt. Otherwise, Lil was okay.

Bending down to collect her purse, the offending stone caught her eye.

In fact, it wasn't a stone at all. Not in the usual sense of the word, at least.

Lil took a step back, clearing the wet leaves with the toe of her shoe.

Squinting, she leaned over to make out an inscription. Then, she rose again and looked out across the clearing.

Other mossy stones peeked out from the bed of leaves, beginning from the base of the narrow path at the back of the rectory and spanning at least a hundred yards onward. They rose above the weeds and wet leaves at odd angles and with no obvious design or pattern. Hodge-podge rows of stones.

And Lil realized what it was she'd stumbled on.

A cemetery. A forgotten, practically *hidden* cemetery.

CHAPTER 15—BETSY

Betsy and Lena had invited the girls over for an after-church luncheon. They needed to get things in gear for the harvest parade, which was just a week out. Bingo, though fun, hadn't resulted in much in the way of Garden Guild chat, so now they were pinched for time.

Betsy hated to be pinched for time. Punctual to a fault, there was no fun to be had if she wasn't duly prepared for it. A quirk that most people would not have attributed to her.

She and her mother scurried home after the service at First Presbyterian of Gull's Landing and a quick stop at the market.

Once home, Betsy grabbed the Sunday paper from the stoop and rushed her mother inside.

Lena took charge of sandwiches. Betsy mixed Arnold Palmers and swapped out last week's bouquet for a fresh set of sunflowers, selected from the store on the way home.

She laid out a notepad at the kitchen table then watered a line of herbs beneath the window that looked out over her lanai.

By the time the sandwiches were set and the glasses poured, Lil and Emily had arrived—together, as Lil had collected the younger girl from the Grimwood home first.

The small group of women, who were fast becoming comfortable with one another, settled in at the table and took to the sandwiches with fervor as Betsy scribbled ideas for their float.

"We can just take the car," she suggested. "Lots of the sponsored floats are just cars with the tops down, you know."

"Won't it be freezing?" Emily wondered aloud.

"It would be freezing even if we were riding on the back of a flatbed," Betsy pointed out.

Lena lifted a crooked finger. "Speaking of flatbeds, Bill has a truck."

All eyes turned to her, but it was Betsy whose cheeks glowed at the mention of the new man in town.

"Bill as in *Greg's* friend?" she asked her mother.

"And our *neighbor*," Lena sang out.

"Can I ask a question here?" Lil interjected, her hand splayed out and her mouth full of sandwich.

Emily giggled, and Betsy shot them both a look, but waved Lil on.

"What's the deal with Greg and this Bill character? Why the tiptoeing? Why the hush-hush? They're just *men*."

Betsy saw Emily's smile dissolve, and she withdrew the newspaper she'd been in charge of bringing, unfolded it and glanced across the front page. Lena buttoned her lips, too.

Left alone to answer, Betsy shrugged. "Exactly," she said. "They're just *men*. We don't need 'em. We'll put the top down on the Reatta and you two skinny ones can perch your little fannies on the back and wave like Miss Americas. Eh 'k?"

"I don't buy it. Not for a second. You, Lena, with the white-haired one, and you, Betsy, with the salt-and-pepper. Why not go for it?"

"There's nothing to *go* for," Lena answered loudly, fanning herself with her napkin. "Greg's old news, and we'll leave it at that."

"Old news?" Betsy cocked an eyebrow.

"Read my lips, *old news.*"

"He moved to The Landing a year ago!" Betsy cried. "That ought to make him hot news. If he's *old* news, well, then... that's news. Ma, *spill*. Now!"

"Speaking of news," Emily chimed in. "Here's the information for the harvest parade." She turned the front page toward the others, and Betsy was grateful for the change in topic.

"Right, right. We need to get down to business. What's our mission, here? Our goal?" she pressed.

"Well," Lil answered, rising from the table to pour herself more lemonade from the bar, "what *is* the goal of the Garden Guild? I mean, what have you girls been up to these last few years?"

Betsy sighed. "Good question."

"Lil, honey," Lena said, "when you were first active in the club, what did you do? What was the schtick?"

"Schtick?" Betsy eyed her mother. "Is that a Greg thing? 'Schtick?'"

Lena pursed her lips and raised her hand to Betsy. "You were saying, Lil?"

"I wasn't saying anything. I mean, I don't know. We took turns meeting at each other's homes where we'd pitch in with ideas on our backyard gardens. That's how I got mine started. The flower part, at least. I've always grown vegetables, you see. We did a few fundraisers for various charities, but I couldn't tell you which ones. I wasn't active then. I mean at *all*. I stuck around for a meeting or two until I found the Canasta gals. Then when they fizzled, I just—stopped doing things with my girlfriends, I suppose. I've never been the sort who's good at making and keeping friends, period."

The others fell quiet at Lil's revelation, and Betsy thought about what she could say. "Well, now you are."

Lil grinned back as she returned to the table. "Yeah. Maybe."

Betsy grabbed Lil's hand across the table and squeezed it then did the same to Emily's. "You two listen. I need some true girlfriends. Not women like Nancy and Pam—sheesh."

"They were never your friends," Lena remarked. "They were hangers-on. Looking for the next bit of gossip, I say. The only friend Betsy has had all her life," the old woman went on, pursing her lips at Lil and Emily, "is me. Wish I could say the same, but I was raised to make friends and *keep* them, you see. And so I have. Women other than my own *daughter* for goodness *sake*." She shook her head.

"Gee thanks, Ma." Betsy rolled her eyes, and laughter rippled across the group. "And if that's true, then I'd like to meet these so-called friends of yours."

"If *you* were my friend, then you'd have met 'em all by now! But no—no. Too busy with work. Too busy with putting together the next floral arrangement or the next *meeting* where you get nothing done!" Lena banged the table lightly with her fists.

Betsy sliced her hand through the air. "I get it. I *get* it! I'm a terrible daughter. Terrible friend to you! Can we *please* focus on the parade so that I can prove to you that we *are* getting something done?"

Lena nodded, her expression casual and nonchalant as ever, and Betsy just chuckled. "Here, Em. Let me see the paper."

Emily passed it over and Betsy laid it out, smoothing the page down on the table before reading aloud from the article. All the details were there. The time. The staging information. Who to contact. All that.

"Okay, so let's back up and talk about this so-called Guild," she began, setting the paper off to the side by her mother and pulling her notepad in front of her. She licked the tip of her pen and scrawled *Garden Guild* across the top of a fresh page.

"Weekly meetings," Lil replied. "We meet each week. Casually or otherwise."

"Great," Betsy answered, adding it to the page. "Rotate houses?" At that, Emily made a sound. The others looked up. "What, Em?"

"I just... I don't *have* a house."

"Just because you don't own the place you live in

doesn't mean you don't *have* a house. I bet ol' Grimwood would love it if you planted some flowers in the front yard there," Betsy answered.

"You know who would love it," Lena pointed out. "That mother of his."

"Do you know her?" Lil asked suddenly, her eyes narrowing on Lena.

"Irma Grimwood?" Lena shook her head. "I know *of* her. From church. She's old, though."

"Ma!" Betsy cried. "Speak for yourself."

"I'd speak for myself if I had to. I'm not old, though. Not compared to Irma Grimwood. She must've had that boy when she was forty, I tell you. She was born last century. Swear to God."

"Regardless," Betsy went on. "We take turns, and we do, you know, garden stuff."

"And as for the parade? What's our plan there?" Lil asked.

"We decorate the Reatta in silk flowers. Each of us can hold a bouquet. And we can have a little sign that reads Gull's Landing Garden Guild." Betsy wrote that down as she said it.

"But what's the point?" Emily asked meekly, hiding the bottom part of her face behind her glass.

"The point?" Betsy echoed.

"The point of the parade? If we aren't recruiting or advertising, or whatever, then what's the point?"

"Oh, honey," Betsy answered. "It's Gull's Landing. The point is simply to *see* and to *be seen*. See? If you're lucky enough to have a club, then you get the chance to parade around town mid-way through November. And since we sometimes host a booth at the harvest festival—hey wait a minute!" Betsy snapped. "That's *it*. Forget the *parade*. We need to focus on our booth!"

"Betsy," her mother groaned. "The festival is for selling wares. And it used to be that the Guild sold fresh vegetables and herbs. You haven't stepped a foot into your own garden in months."

"I've only got one pumpkin," Lil pointed out.

Betsy stood and crossed to the window. "My herbs don't count?" she held her hand like the pretty girl from *Wheel of Fortune*, indicating each fresh, healthy spray of green gleaming against the afternoon sun.

"Focus on the parade. Save the festival for next year, when you have an actual... *you know*... harvest."

"Lena has a point," Lil said. "We'll do the parade. The flowers. Garland, maybe. Fall foliage. And it'll be our jumping off point. Our coming out party, if you will."

"Fine." Betsy sighed. "In that case, I suppose we need to meet a few times this week to start decorations. Then on Saturday, we'll need to get there early to deck the Reatta." Betsy squinted at her notepad. She'd forgotten to write down the check-in time. "What time do the cars line up on Elm, again?"

Lena grabbed the copy of Gull's Gazette and read the details aloud again as Betsy jotted them down. "So we meet at eight o'clock Saturday morning at the top of Elm and First Street. Agreed?" Betsy flashed a look at each of them. Lil and Emily nodded as Lil studied Betsy's kitchen counter—a neat line of cookbooks wedged between ceramic bookends.

"We could make some baked goods, too. There's a

spot at the end of the parade where you can sit in your car and pass out gifts or goodies. If we *do* want to recruit, or at least make ourselves 'seen,' as you say, then we could make some pumpkin pie. Zucchini bread. Use fresh ingredients. Maybe head to the pumpkin patch just outside town. We can pick our own gourds and legumes."

A gasp came from Lena's corner of the table, and the other three sets of eyes flew to her.

"Ma, what is it?"

The paper lowered in front of the old woman's face, her red lips forming a perfect oh. "Have any of you seen *this*?" She folded the paper back, flipped it around, and folded it once more, stabbing with a finger at a black-and-white photograph of none other than Nancy Shytle and her husband, Roy. Nancy Shytle, *former* Garden Guild member who was *supposed* to be occupied that month. Out of town. Or burdened with company. Betsy couldn't remember which. Just that she was decidedly unavailable for the parade.

Betsy squinted at the article, reaching for it when she couldn't make it out across the short distance.

She read the headline aloud for the others, "Local Business Owners Propose Second Cemetery."

"What?" Lil cried from across the table.

Betsy cleared her throat and went on. "Proprietors of Gull's Landing Gambling Hall, *Nancy* and Roy Shytle call into question the growing need for a greater capacity when it comes to local options for the deceased and their families."

"Oh, yeah," Emily chimed in, her voice full of awe and

remembrance. "Mr. Grimwood mentioned something about that."

"What do you mean?" Lil asked Emily then turned her head to Betsy. "What else does it say?"

Betsy read again. "The Shytles will make a proposal to develop and run a public cemetery. They're eying property just south of town, between Elm Street and Maple, on a tract of land previously used for medical offices. Their proposal would include significant infrastructural changes to the south end of Gull's Landing, but as the Shytles say, 'Second Street Mortuary is nearly at its limit. In ten or twenty years, who knows what could happen? Local families may be forced to lie in rest in a different town altogether, and we just can't have that. Not when we are a close-knit, family-focused community.'" Betsy looked up. "Wow," she said, lowering the paper. "When did she decide to go and do a thing like *that*?"

Lil reached for the paper. "May I see that?"

Betsy handed it off. "Emily, what do you mean Grimwood mentioned it? He *knows* about this? Are they in on it together? Are the Shytles—what—his investors or something?"

She shrugged. "I don't know. I don't *think* so. He seemed—bothered. Upset."

"Of course he'd be upset." Lil glowered from behind the Gazette. "They're going to take his business."

"It's a real issue, though," Lena reasoned. "What happens when Second Street is full of dead bodies?"

"*Ma*," Betsy hissed. "There's no way Second Street is even close to capacity. It's got plenty of plots left. We were just there. I saw for myself."

"It seems cramped to me," Emily piped up.

Betsy gave her a look, and she shrank back.

Lil just shook her head and disappeared back behind the paper. "How can they know it's at capacity, anyway? What—did they conduct an *audit* or something?" She peeked out over top of the paper at Emily who, again, shrugged.

"I've always wondered about that sort of thing. Not for myself, necessarily. I don't much care what you do with my body." Lena preened.

"Lena," Lil said, "isn't your husband buried at Second Street?"

"John? No. Milwaukee. Cost an arm and a leg to ship him out there, too," Lena answered.

Betsy covered her face in her hands. "*Mother.*"

"I just want fresh flowers and green grass. Wherever you put me. In a tin can or a golden tomb—fresh flowers. Is that so much to ask?" Lena grumbled.

"And fresh flowers you will *get*, Lena," Lil answered. "At Second Street Mortuary."

"Norman should fight it," Betsy said, folding her arms over her bosom. "He should fight the Shytles."

"What do you mean?" Lil asked. Dropping the paper to the table.

"When Travel by Tracy came crawling into town, she had the decency to come to our agency and discuss the possibility of opening a storefront on First Street. We told her the idea wouldn't serve our business *or* hers. So, she went further down the shore. And I think she's happy and successful as hell. The Shytles, they should have talked to Norman. Gone in together, at the very least. Or inquired about if he wanted to. Did he want to, Lil?"

Lil blanched. "Well, I have *no* idea. It's not as though I *talk* to Norman Grimwood." She laughed mildly and glanced again at the article.

Betsy pursed her lips. "I'm telling you, Lil." She looked at Emily. "And you, Em. Talk to Norman. Tell him to fight the proposal."

Lil pointed at the article. "It says here they'll be presenting their plan at the town council meeting on Tuesday."

Betsy nodded gravely. "Then Norman Grimwood needs to be at that council meeting. And so does anyone who supports him."

CHAPTER 16—EMILY

Mr. Grimwood was nearly late to the funeral home on Monday.

When Emily had left the house, there was no sign of either him or Mrs. Grimwood. At first, Emily wondered if perhaps Norman had gone into the funeral home early, and so she left at her usual time, picking her way across the frost-slick sidewalk to the mortuary, where she used her key to let herself in.

Once inside, however, she found the lights off—the lobby and Mr. Grimwood's office empty.

Upon further inspection, Emily discovered that the mortician, Mr. Krueger, was already at work, cleaning the preparation room, as was his usual chore on Monday mornings, assuming he had no remains to see to.

Emily bid him well and returned to the lobby to find Mr. Grimwood fumbling to close the front door as he tried again and again to get the latch to catch.

"Mr. Grimwood," she said, confused at the sight of him—nervous and odd-acting. "Is everything okay?"

"The latch," he answered, his voice rattling uncontrollably. "This *damn* old *door* and its faulty latch!" His voice roared higher, and Emily took a step back, paling.

Mr. Grimwood's face turned beet red and he let the door be, unlatched and creeping open second by second. "Emily," he whispered, wiping his forehead with the back of his hand. "I'm terribly sorry."

She remained perfectly still, waiting for him to step closer. Or to leave. Or to do something as out of the ordinary as his momentary temper tantrum.

"It's Mother," he stammered, his voice shaky all over again.

Emily's body relaxed. "Mrs. Grimwood?" she asked lamely.

He nodded. "She—she had a bad night. The doctor is coming to the house to check on her. She's—she's *sick*, you see. And I think she's had a terrible turn."

Emily took a step forward. "Oh, Mr. Grimwood. I didn't realize. I'm—I'm sorry to hear this. What can I do? Can I go there and be with her for his visit? Whatever you'd like, I'll do it."

His shoulders dropped and his face broke. The man pushed two fingers into his eye sockets and heaved a shuddering sigh. "No, no, Emily. That won't be necessary. I'll make my way back there just as soon as I finish a little work here. She's in good hands. It's—nothing *new*, I hate to say."

"She's been sick for a while?" Emily asked, wondering about the woman's cough. Her feebleness. Paleness.

Mr. Grimwood nodded miserably. "Lung cancer."

Emily's heart sank. "I had no idea."

"Anyway, as I said. I just need to finish some paperwork from the Devlin funeral, then I'm heading straight back."

"Mr. Grimwood," Emily said before he could duck away into his office. "I hate to pester you about this, but I figured you'd like to know..."

"Yes, Emily?" his voice read impatience and his face turned wan, but Emily wanted to follow Betsy's directions. And besides, she figured Mr. Grimwood would want to know.

"Tomorrow night the town council meets, you see."

He waited, pressing his lips into a thin line.

"And the—the *Shytles* will be there. With their proposal to open a new cemetery."

Mr. Grimwood grimaced and stretched his neck left then right, rolling his head around in a circle at last. "Right. Yes. I saw that."

"My friend," Emily went on, testing the word out to see if it fit. It did. "My friend, Betsy Borden, you see, she knows about business things, and, well, she thinks it's important that you fight the proposal, Mr. Grimwood."

He frowned. "Fight the proposal?"

Emily nodded seriously. "Yes, sir. And, we will all be there. Betsy, me, Betsy's mother, and even Lil Gulch. We'll be there to back you, Mr. Grimwood."

"What do you mean?" He shifted his weight in the doorframe, leaning against the wood as his expression softened from confusion to mild interest.

"We don't agree with what she's doing, this Nancy Shytle woman. And her husband, Roy. We think it's terribly wrong, and we want to support you. That's all."

Mr. Grimwood shook his head. "But they're right. The Shytles. Second Street has another ten years of clients, at the outside. After that, we'll be full. Maybe even before ten years. Depending."

"But you're the funeral director in town. It's your *business*," Emily pled. "I work here, too, and Nancy is just wrong to do it. She ought to have talked to you first, Mr. Grimwood."

"And Betsy Borden thinks I have a chance against the Shytles? The owners of the gambling hall?" He let out another heavy sigh. "I don't, Emily. And I've got more important *business* right now." Mr. Grimwood disappeared into his office, and Emily felt bad for him.

She had nothing more to add. Nothing else to work with to convince him to save his own business. And besides, she didn't know exactly why Betsy and Lil were so worked up about Nancy Shytle and her husband, Roy. Why did they care if Norman Grimwood had competition? Especially if Mr. Grimwood himself didn't seem to mind?

"Emily?" Mr. Grimwood poked his head out from his office, his face earnest.

"Yes, sir?"

"The town council meeting," he went on, his voice soft and worrisome. "What time does it start?"

CHAPTER 17—LIL

It was none of Lil's business. It was none of Betsy's business or Lena's. Or Emily's.

Well, the success of the Second Street Mortuary *was* Emily's business, since she worked there.

But whether the Second Street Mortuary *or* cemetery floundered—whether they met with steep competition —*that* was *not* Lil's business.

However, it was Nancy Shytle who was behind the issue. Nancy Shytle and her husband, Roy. Nancy, the one woman in the world whom Lil could say she *loathed*. That was a big thing, since Lil wasn't one to hate anyone. She really wasn't.

Lil mainly appeared for the town council meeting out of curiosity. And Betsy's urging.

It had fast become clear that Betsy was a bulldozer of a woman, and Lil liked that about her. A bulldozer for good. Who couldn't appreciate a woman who made things happen?

She wrapped herself in a warm cable knit sweater the

color of mustard, slipped into her winter boots, and contemplated calling Emily. The awkward thing about Emily's living situation was that she didn't have her own phone line. She used the Grimwood house phone. What if Norman answered? What would Lil say? *Hi, Norman. Lil Gulch, here. Listen, I'd like to come get Emily and take her to that council meeting that has to do with the future of your funeral business...*

No.

She'd come across as... *interested*. Or even *very* interested.

Could she be vague, however? She *could* be, yes.

Picking up the receiver, Lil referenced her address book before dragging the numbers across the dial in long arcs.

One ring in, a croaking woman answered. "Hello?" she asked, coughing into the line.

Lil waited a beat then replied. "Hi, Mrs. Grimwood? This is Lil Gulch. Lillian Gulch. You might remember me from—"

"Lillian, yes, of course." A wheezing sound cut the poor woman off momentarily. "You're calling for Norman, I'd imagine."

"Oh, no, Mrs. Grimwood. I, um, I'm calling for Emily Addams. Is she home? Or, rather, is she there?"

"Emily? Why, yes. Yes. I'll just get her. Won't you please wait?"

Lil said she would and tapped her foot on the parquet floor of her kitchen. Some moments later, after muffled conversation and another round of coughing in the background, Emily came on the line.

"Lil?"

"Emily, hi. Is *she* okay?"

"Who?" Emily asked. "Mrs. Grimwood?"

"Yes, she sounds... sick?"

"She is." The reply was clipped, and before Lil could gather details, Emily added, "Um, are you calling about the council meeting?"

"Yes," Lil answered. "I wondered if you might like to join me. Betsy's going, and I figure I'd like to see what Nancy has up her sleeve—"

"Mr. Grimwood is driving me, in fact."

"Oh." Lil's breath hitched. "So, he *is* going?"

"Yes. I spoke with him about it, and then I mentioned it to his mother. She encouraged him, too," Emily said. Her voice dropped. "I've got to go now, Lil. I'll meet you at the meeting. We can save you a seat."

Lil's heart thudded in her chest. She knew Nancy. Knew her well enough to know that Norman's arrival with a pretty young girl would add fuel to the woman's fire. "Wait, Emily. Meet me outside. All right? Just—just don't go *in* with Norman."

But it was too late. The line had already gone dead.

LIL WASTED no time in driving to the town hall. Her best chance of thwarting further conflict would be to arrive ahead of everyone—Nancy, Norman, and Emily. Then, once she spotted them, she could pull Emily aside and let Norman go in alone. Or even, maybe, Lil would join them. If Norman entered with an entourage, then Nancy could see that and maybe back down. But it had to be all or none. The worst thing would be if Norman entered the building with a single woman by his side. Nancy would sic him like a dog.

Having never attended a town council meeting, Lil didn't know what to expect once she parked and strode to the front steps. Scarce few attendees trickled past her. One seemingly married couple and a handful of single-tons. The council members themselves—or, at least, who Lil *thought* were the council members—arrived amongst the general public. Before she knew it, it was five minutes to six and Lil hadn't seen Nancy (or her husband) *or* Norman and Emily walk in. Betsy and Lena were missing, too.

She glanced at her watch. Four minutes to six.

A shiver rattled her body and hunger pains struck her abdomen. Lil hadn't been great about eating in the last few weeks. Nothing sounded good. She picked at food, filling up on beverages in lieu of real nutrition.

"Lillian Gulch." Her name seeped like poison through the chilly night air.

Lil squinted into the darkness to see Nancy Shytle and her husband, Roy, mounting the steep cliff of stairs to the town hall building.

"Nancy, hello," Lil replied smoothly, pulling her sweater more tightly around her body. "I hear you have some grand plans for the town." As the sentence left her mouth, Lil wished she could have pulled it back. Showing her hand would only hurt, not help.

"Oh!" Nancy laughed warmly. "Oh, Lillian. That's kind of you. Well," she paused, her arm laced daintily through her husband's, "I would agree they are *grand*. But you know, Lillian—I mean... *surely* you of all people *know* how crowded Second Street is. I mean, *really*, Lillian. Your poor Sam. He's squeezed in there between an old Civil War hero and the entire Jameson clan. The place is choking with remains." Her eyes turned wet. "I can't fathom what will become of us, Lillian. I really can't."

She was a different woman, this Nancy, on the arm of her dud of a husband.

Lil hadn't noticed who Sam was interred between. Was it really a war hero? And the Jamesons? Who were they? Nancy's attempt to one-up, no doubt. Prove who was the *true* local. The one who cared *more*. *Most*, even.

"Anywho," Nancy pushed ahead when Lil didn't reply. "See you in there." Her smile turned to ice, and Lil felt herself tremble in the woman's wake.

"Lil!" In the distance, she could just make out the figures of a man and a slight woman getting out of a car and heading toward the steps.

Norman and Emily.

Lil forced herself to let out the breath she'd been holding as she waved to them.

Safe. With Nancy inside, they were safe.

"We'd better hurry," Lil warned. "It's nearly six, and you'll have to sign in if you want to speak at the Call to the Public."

Norman looked uneasy. Restless and fidgety.

"Are we all speaking?" Emily asked, her face worry-filled, too.

Lil shook her head. "Betsy and Lena aren't here. At least, I haven't seen them. I figure it's best if you spearhead this, Norman." She looked at him. "You do want to present a counter argument, I assume."

Their relationship wasn't even quite that—a relationship. Lil had no idea what Norman thought of her. All she knew was what she thought of him—a kindly man. Her age. Her speed. Gentle of voice and action. That was it. That was all she had.

So why did she care so much whether Nancy Shytle and her husband, Roy, opened a second cemetery or not?

Sam was already dead and buried and squashed between dead strangers. Lil might save herself the hassle and just vanish into the night, even. Or she could have her own remains shipped off to Philly, when the time came. What did it matter to her if there was space so many years from now?

Then again, there was a longing that kept her there. A longing to overcome the past—to overcome her conflict with Nancy. And a longing to make something work, there, in Gull's Landing. A longing to see what the future held. A longing to see about this Norman character and what might be in store for the two of them. Then again—perhaps nothing would be in store. Perhaps that particular longing was for a thin, diluted potential that probably only existed in Lil's fantasies.

And then there was Emily. Sweet-natured Emily, new to town just like Lil had been. Settling in, just like Lil had. To rip the rug out from beneath a new friend... Lil knew better than to allow that. Especially if that rug was at the hands of a veritable enemy.

Nancy *was* an enemy. This became clearer by the day.

Norman stuffed his fists into his pockets, withdrew

one immediately, scratched the back of his head, stuffed it back into his pocket and looked at Lil. "I'm not quite sure what to say, truth be told."

She blinked. "Oh. Well…" Lil licked her lips. "Norman —Mr. Grimwood—do you… are you in favor of the Shytles opening a new mortuary?"

"It's just a cemetery they intend to open, I believe." He twisted his lips into a tight knot. "Though I could be wrong about that."

Lil glanced at her watch. The meeting was set to begin presently. "Norman," her voice dropped, "listen. Will your business survive if it's split down the middle? If you took in half the clients you do now, would it survive? If you only ran funeral services but no burials, would you survive?"

"Well, no, Lillian—Lil—but then again, I doubt that a new mortuary operation, or even just a cemetery, would take off in the first place." He scratched his head. "This town is too small for two mortuaries. Or *cemeteries*, as the case may be."

"Then *that* is what you say." She patted his shoulder, wishing they had the brazen Betsy Borden to speak on their behalf.

CHAPTER 18—LIL

"Lil!"

As Lil, Norman, and Emily stepped in through the doors together, she spotted Betsy and Lena, sitting in the back row. Betsy had hissed her name at a volume just above a stage whisper, and the entire room had glanced back to see the odd trio. Even Nancy stared, and Lil watched her lean in and whisper something to Roy in the front row.

They shuffled into the plastic chairs provided for the monthly gatherings, and Betsy gave Lil a knowing look.

As the meeting unfolded, Betsy passed a typed-up agenda, of sorts, to Lil. The only item, after the pledge and a review of the town budget, was the Shytles' proposal. After that, the Call to the Public. Lil sucked in a breath and passed the page to Norman, who sat bouncing his leg in the seat beside her.

After a drawn-out summary of money spent and money earned, it was Nancy's turn.

She stood, her back rigid and her sinewy hands—

French-tipped and bejeweled—clinging to a stack of packets.

Lil imagined those hands—those fingers—in another context. Doing worse things than flipping Tarot cards. The hands of a witch, Lil decided. A malevolent, sinister witch of a woman.

After passing one to each councilmember, Nancy took her spot at the podium, which was positioned at an angle to the front but not to such a degree that Nancy couldn't easily lift a hand and indicate the poor, helpless audience—her *victims*, as Lil considered them, herself included.

"Thank you, Mayor and council members. My name is Nancy Shytle, and I'm here tonight on behalf of my husband, Roy, and myself as well as the good towns-people of Gull's Landing." She flashed a sugary smile to the modest crowd of "townspeople."

Betsy snorted next to Lil.

"Go on, Mrs. Shittle," the mayor answered, and Nancy visibly glowered.

"*Shytle*," she corrected him but not before a low rumble of chuckles bubbled across the room. Even Nancy's own correction still sounded an awful lot like, well, *Shittle*. The difference, Lil could scarcely tell, was in the Y. Not quite a short I sound, as in *insect*, but not quite a long I sound, as in *Ice Queen*.

"Anyway," Nancy chirped, shaking her potato-brown hair from her shoulders and pasting another smile across her mouth. "As many of you know, Roy and I own and operate the Gull's Landing Gambling Hall. We've lived here in town for over twenty years, and we've seen great

success in our entrepreneurial and *charitable* endeavors."
She smirked at her husband who, Lil could have sworn,
flashed a thumbs up from his hip. "We love Gull's
Landing and its people, and we intend to spend the rest
of our lives here." Her smile dropped abruptly. "Which
brings me to my next point." She took a deep, dramatic
breath in and folded her hands neatly on the podium.
"Mayor and council members, I, as well as a few of the
good citizens in attendance tonight—" she passed one
hand back—toward Lil, no doubt, "—had the misfortune
of burying one of our own just recently." If Lil didn't
know any better, she'd have thought Nancy's voice broke.
A hairline fissure—a chink in the façade. Lil narrowed
her gaze on the woman, who had paused either for effect
or out of sincerity. It was impossible to tell which.

The mayor took a hint and filled in the blank. He
didn't know Lil or Sam, and they didn't know the mayor,
but what he said next was a nice enough thought. "Our
condolences are with Mrs. Gulch," he grumbled into the
microphone, dipping his first chin into his second and
third chins sympathetically.

Lil's cheeks flushed. She had *not* intended to be a
focus of the evening's narrative. Still, she nodded, swallowing past a thick lump in her throat. Betsy squeezed
her arm. Norman's hand trembled on his knee and
glanced at her, his eyes soft.

"Indeed," Nancy agreed from the podium. "*Tragic*,"
she added as a whisper. But her recovery was swift, and
she pushed ahead. "I had the honor of attending Sam
Gulch's funeral, and while the Second Street Mortuary
provided a very nice service, Mayor and council

members, you might agree when I point out just how *small* the cemetery is. I noticed that there would hardly be room for Sam's late wife to join him, there, near his plot."

Lil stifled a grunt.

"Which brings me to my proposal. Roy and I would like to establish a second cemetery on the south side of town in the old medical offices' plaza. As both a new business—to help *stoke* the local economy, *and*—" Nancy pressed her hand to her chest and lowered her chin, closing her eyes "—as a service to the fine people of Gull's Landing. Every citizen has a right to be laid to rest in his or *her* hometown." She opened her eyes and smiled, her speech complete.

The room was silent enough to hear a pin drop. After a beat, Roy Shytle clapped dully from his seat in the front row, the sound echoing off the wood-paneled walls.

The mayor cleared his throat. "Thank you, Mrs. Shittle." He looked at the other council members who nodded appreciatively.

Nancy smirked. "On a final note, you'll see a breakdown of the acreage and square footage of the current Second Street Cemetery as well as our proposed property south of town. I've also taken the liberty of counting the current gravesites at Second Street and prevised an estimate, based on current annual death rates, of how many plots Second Street will be able to sustain. I regret to note that *something* must happen, Mayor. Council Members." She flicked a quick look to the back of the room, her gaze landing momentarily and purposefully on Lil, for whatever reason. "And *soon*."

Nancy shook her hair back and rounded the podium, shuffling haughtily back to her seat.

Next to Lil, poor Norman let out a heavy sigh and drew his hands to his face, rubbing his eyes.

"Again, thank you." The mayor slid his packet away and clasped his hands behind his microphone. "Now for the Call to the Public. I see we have one person signed up. Is that right?"

"Oh no," Lil hissed. "We didn't get a chance—" but before she could raise her hand or rise and dash to the front of the room on Norman's behalf, Betsy stood up.

"That's right, your, um, your honor." A cascade of laughter came on the heels of her flub, and Lil eased back in her seat, smiling at her friend. "So sorry," Betsy corrected. "*Mayor*."

She made her way up to the podium, gripping the microphone and launching immediately into a brash response to Nancy Shytle.

"Betsy Borden," she began. "Former owner and president of Book with Borden. President of the Gull's Landing Garden Guild. Concerned citizen," Betsy continued, leaning heavily on the hollow-core wood, her lips grazing the microphone screen.

Norman leaned into Lil, whispering into her ear. "What is she going to say?" His breath was hot and caught on tendrils of her hair, tickling her and sending a chill down her spine.

Lil pursed her lips and inhaled through her nose before shaking her head and whispering back, "Who knows?"

"Pursuant to local laws, it is wholly unnecessary for a

new cemetery to be erected in town," Betsy went on, her word choice striking an almost humorous tone. Lil prayed silently she'd tone it down.

"What local laws?" the mayor interrupted.

"Well," Betsy continued, "when Book with Borden proposed a new office building on Fifth Street, on vacant land, mind you, we were rejected. Do you know why?" Betsy held her palm up toward Nancy, but she didn't wait for an answer. "Because of the infrastructural overhaul it would entail. The council members at the time asked us to first seek a previously erected structure and make use of that, where possible. In fact, that *was* possible, and we moved into the storefront available on Fourth Street. From my brief research into the development of a brand new cemetery, I found that Gull's Landing might take a similar response to the Shytles. You see, a cemetery affects the groundwater, potentially. It's *always* best to make use of current designated burial grounds before disrupting, significantly in this case, intact infrastructure. And what's more, it has come to my attention that Nancy Shytle and her husband, Roy, didn't bother to first consult our resident funeral director who just so happens to own the town's lone, active cemetery, the Second Street Cemetery." Betsy pointed a finger at Norman and Lil shrank half an inch away from him. "Norman Grimwood."

Murmurs lifted across the modest crowd and eyes turned on them.

To his credit, Norman raised a hand and waved to the council, nodding and keeping his gaze steely.

"Mr. Grimwood," the mayor said, "Would you mind if

we pose a few brief questions to you? In the interest of a timely response to the Shittles' proposal?"

"Not at all, sir." Norman stood, pushing his hands deep into his pockets and leveling his chin with the ground. Lil's eyes wandered up his form and landed on the back of his head—the short-shorn hair flecked with silver and spreading evenly over his head. The clean line of his haircut at the top of his neck. Everything about him was clean and even and *honest*. Her chest clenched.

"Miss Borden, if you're done, you may sit." The mayor cleared his throat into his microphone and Betsy thanked him before striding back to their row and winking conspicuously at Lil on her way.

Lil forced herself to ignore it as she sat there, nervous for Norman. Nervous for herself too, for some reason.

"Mr. Grimwood, tell us: are Mrs. Shittle's figures accurate? Is your capacity as strained as she suggests?"

Norman gave a short nod in response. "Her numbers seem accurate to me, sir. Although, it's hard to predict what the future holds for the residents of Gull's Landing. Who moves away. Who moves in. Who opts for cremation." He pulled his hands from his pockets, folded them in front of himself, and rolled his shoulders back and down. Lil could see the muscles in his back through the thin fabric of his cotton shirt. For a quiet, middle-aged funeral director, he had a surprisingly fit body. Better than Sam's, Lil estimated.

"And is it true the Shittles didn't first approach you about their idea to expand our... *options*?" The mayor danced around the topic at hand, which Lil found a little funny.

Norman nodded again. "That's true, sir." Lil silently urged him to say more. To say what he'd said to her—it was a bad business, this Shytle mess, and if Norman wanted to preserve his business—his *livelihood*, he needed to be more aggressive. Lil braced for popping out of her seat. Even if it was out of turn.

But the mayor prompted him again. Evidently trying to help. "Mr. Grimwood, what *are* your thoughts on a second cemetery? Is Nancy's prediction correct? Do we... well... *need* another one? And if so, what does that mean for our so-called infrastructure? Could it poison our water? Disrupt the traffic patterns?" The mayor loosened his tie, settling into his seat as he switched his tone.

"It's true that we may need more space in the coming decade. Or two. But I can tell you this—if a second cemetery opens, it won't be bringing 'new business' to town. We'll split the business. And though yes, the funeral and cemetery industry can be a sure bet, it's not *lucrative* by any stretch of the imagination. As for infrastructure, you're looking at a big interruption, I'd expect."

Nancy's brown hair flashed as her head spun. "The future of Gull's Landing depends on a *second* cemetery, Norman."

"Enough." The mayor tapped the microphone. "I'll review the Second Street Cemetery. Walk it. Measure it. What*ever*," he went on, exasperated, no doubt. "And if it turns out we need more space, we'll re-address the proposal. Save your comments and questions for my secretary who will schedule the walk-through."

And like *that*, it was over. The meeting was done and a cool, early winter breeze had carried everyone out of the wood-paneled room, depositing them back, in a little huddle, on the front landing, like churchgoers who'd just gone and were ready to *go* but stood lingering, shaking hands with acquaintances, thanking the priest, wondering about doughnuts and coffee in the family hall.

Nancy Shytle and her husband, Roy, sniffed the air as they squeezed through Lil and her group of friends, adding as they descended the steps, "Locals have a right to a *local* burial."

Lil wanted desperately to spit something sharp and cutting back at Nancy, but the night swallowed her quickly and by then, all Lil could do was slump against the railing.

"Who does she think she is?" Betsy asked. "I'm *glad* she's out of the Guild. What a horrid woman. Why didn't I see it sooner?"

Emily agreed through a nod. "It seems like she's *trying* to make an enemy."

"My money's on trouble in paradise," Betsy ventured.

Lil frowned. "As in... with their marriage?"

"Marriage? Hah. That's not a marriage. And no, I meant with their *business*. Why else is she scamming on poor ol' Norm, here?" Betsy patted Norman on the shoulder.

But Lil knew better. Nancy's little plot had nothing to do with business. Or her marriage.

It was personal.

And it had to do with Lil.

CHAPTER 19—BETSY

The week flew by. The girls got together three times to create their banners and configure their floral arrangements for the parade.

Come Saturday morning, Betsy felt ready. She didn't know exactly *what* she was ready for—this would be her first year heading up the Garden Guild float. But she was ready.

They met at eight on the nose, working quickly to affix the banners to either side of the Reatta before securing fanciful autumnal arrangements to every part of the car where they could possibly fasten a bouquet. Sunflowers and mums dominated the décor, splashing yellows and reds, browns and oranges at every angle.

When it was time to coast down First Street, Betsy's nerves hit. She was driving. Lena was in the passenger seat. Lil and Emily rode on the back, tossing carnations into the road in lieu of candy as they hummed along between people-lined sidewalks from Elm all the way to Boardwalk Boulevard. All eyes were on the Reatta. On the banners—*Gull's Landing Garden Guild*, simple, tasteful. They were simply *there*. Part of a special seasonal moment in town.

Betsy recalled the years she had spent on her father's float as a girl, waving to the blurred faces, kids on their fathers' shoulders. Betsy had never been a kid on her father's shoulders. She'd been a kid in the back office. A kid at his desk. A kid flipping through coloring books on the carpet of the sales floor. A kid hawking travel packages on the flatbed of a harvest parade float by chucking little candies to the crowd—candies wrapped in plastic that read, "Book with Borden! Call today!"

As she rested her hand on the steering wheel, waving occasionally to the onlookers, Betsy realized she may have made a mistake. What was life now? With no *career*? No more *legacy*? Was this *it*? A florally outfitted drive down First Street to represent a gardening club that hadn't picked up a watering can in at least two seasons? Had her mother been onto something?

A wave of heat climbed up Betsy's back. She could feel red patches materializing around her neck like a choker.

"What'sa matter?" Lena asked over the beat of the Gull's Landing High Marching Band.

Betsy rolled her eyes. "*Ma*, geez. *Nothing*. Can't you enjoy a drive in a parade without nagging me?"

"Your neck is splotchy. You're *stressed*, Bets. What'sa matter?"

"Nothing." Betsy threw her head back and shook out her hair, freeing herself of the inner feelings of guilt. There'd be something else. A different opportunity.

Another chance to be on top again. In the business world —where she belonged.

The rest of the ride, Betsy was forced to continue to convince her mother that she was *fine*, just a hot flash. Naturally, Lena accused her of being too young for hot flashes, which Betsy jumped on. "I'll remember you said this next time you tell me my eggs are shriveling up inside of my body."

"You can be young and old at the same time. Look at me."

"I'm just thinking about what's next, Ma. That's all."

"What's next? Whatdya mean, what's next? We get the hell outta here and get a hot toddy at the club."

IT WASN'T until the very end, when the parade participants were corralled in the parking lot of Pelican Pier, that Betsy realized the boardwalk amusement park had its very own float, too. A garish, towering thing manned by an unfamiliar stranger. Sitting on the sides of the flatbed back were none other than Greg Rosen and Bill, the new neighbor.

The girls bounced out of her car, each of them hungry and thirsty and tired, but Betsy tried to rein them back in, hoping desperately to avoid Bill and Greg.

"Let's go to the club. Lunch is on me."

"Yeah, okay, Ma," Betsy agreed with her mother's suggestion easily, happy for the diversion. Anyway, it was a good idea to grab something to eat, too.

"Aren't those the guys from Bingo?" Emily pointed to

the backs of two men as they walked around Maeve's café float. Her voice was too loud.

Betsy threw her a look. "Ma wants to go to the club for a drink and a bite," she answered sharply.

"Yeah, it's Bill," Lil agreed. "And he's with the other one—Lena's friend."

"Let's leave. *Now*. Girls, get back in here," Lena croaked, and Betsy's edge softened. It *was* interesting to watch her mother squirm about Greg Rosen.

Betsy had met Greg Rosen just the year before, when he showed up to a clubhouse event jangling loose change in his pocket, whistling pleasantries through his teeth, and plucking cucumber slices from a veggie tray. Betsy had been there without her mother, for once, and had immediately warmed to the kindly older man, introducing herself and welcoming him to the community cheerfully. And it was easy, too. Greg had lived in Gull's Landing years before, returning to retire and settle back in his hometown after taking a teaching assignment in New England for the better part of his life, he'd said. He seemed to just... fit in. Right away. Like he *knew* everyone. Even Betsy.

Later, when Betsy bumped into Greg again, this time *with* Lena, there was no need for an introduction. Lena had known Greg, apparently, from her childhood in Gull's Landing. She didn't *hate* him, she swore. He was *nothing* to her, she swore.

Betsy knew better, but she'd never pressed the issue.

And currently, she happened to agree about skedaddling out of there. Bill irritated Betsy in much the same way as Greg seemed to irritate Lena.

But once she finally managed to pull the car through a narrow space between Maeve's float and the toy store's float, someone else pulled out in front of them. A BMW, as red as Betsy's Reatta but prettier. Sleeker. Newer. *Hotter*.

Betsy scowled. "Who in the world does this jerk think he is? Tourist. Mark my words."

"What's Norman up to today?" Lil asked Emily in the backseat. Betsy flicked a glance to the rearview mirror and Lil shrugged. "I'm just curious. I mean—after that council meeting, you know? Does he have a walk-through planned with the mayor yet?"

Emily replied, "Yes, as a matter of fact. The mayor comes out on Monday morning."

"Will you accompany them, Em?" Betsy asked.

She answered, "Yes. I'm to take notes. "

"You'll have to report back," Lil replied. "We're all *in* this. You know?"

Betsy nodded to the two reflections in her mirror. "Lil's right. We're *involved* now."

"Why *are* you involved?" Lena asked, shifting in her seat and smirking at Betsy.

"Oh, *Ma*, don't you get it?" Betsy cried. "Nothing happens in this town. And what with the sale of the business, it's nice to be a part of something." As she said it, Betsy realized it was true. She *needed* something, even if it was to be a spectator to the drama with the mortuary. She needed it like she needed air. The stakes. The entertainment. The boiling of small-town intrigue.

"Emily's job could be on the line, Lena," Lil pointed out.

"Oh, that's right." Lena twisted around, gripping the side of her leather seat. "How's that *going*?" she half-whispered. "What with Irma so *sick*. Is Norman a real pill? He must be terribly stressed."

"Irma?" Betsy asked.

"Irma Grimwood. Norm's *mother*," Lena answered.

Betsy shook her head. "How you know everyone in this town is beyond me."

"How wouldn't I know everyone? I'm *from* here. I *go* places. I *do* things." Lena chuckled to herself.

"What's she sick with?" Betsy asked Emily, but again it was her own mother who answered.

"Lung cancer. Smoking. She quit years ago, but it was too late, I guess you could say. It's a sin, I tell you."

"The smoking?" Emily piped up from the back.

"No, not the *smoking*," Lena waved her off. "The *cancer*. Just a sin, I tell you."

Betsy shook her head. "Poor thing. And Norman, too. What a tragedy."

"She's not dead yet," Lil pointed out.

"True," Betsy agreed. "But if she's seeing doctors and doing poorly, well, all the more reason he needs a little help. And the Garden Guild has no charitable projects upcoming. I say we take him on."

"As a club?" Lil asked. "We can do that—like, *sponsor* him?"

"Sure," Betsy said. "And you know what—I'll do you one better."

She pulled to a stop outside the gate of The Landing, punching her security code into the metal box. "I'll help, too."

"What do you mean, you'll help?" Lena cried. "What're you gonna do?"

Betsy pulled through the gate as it stretched open automatically. She glanced in her sideview mirror to see a second red car come up behind her, squeezing into the community just before the gate started to close again.

"Hey," she cried. "There's that Beemer again. He's *following* us in!" Betsy pushed the brakes and glared into her mirror, leveling her stare on the man in the driver's seat. "Oh my Lord," she groaned. "It's *him*."

"Who?" Lena squinted into the passenger side mirror. "And how did they get *behind* us, anyway? Were you speeding, Betsy?"

"*Bill*," Betsy answered. "What a scumbag, trailing in on my security code."

"Doesn't he live here?" Emily offered meekly.

Betsy shook her head. "Well, yes, he *lives* here, but—"

"But what? He's good looking, Betsy," Lil pointed out uselessly.

"I don't care how good he looks or how fancy his car is or if he lives in The Landing. Only a scumbag tails a woman into her own neighborhood."

Betsy was heated as she pulled into the roundabout that would take her to the clubhouse and away from Bill. What a lowlife, she thought. Really and truly. A handsome, obviously successful, *charming* lowlife. They existed. They did. But what did Bill have that Betsy didn't?

"He's a lawyer for Pelican Pier, I heard," Lena said. "Who knew a theme park hired its own lawyers?"

"That's *it*." Betsy snapped her fingers once she put the car in park.

"What?" the other three asked all at once. Lena, the most alarmed.

"I'm going back to work," Betsy answered.

"Doing *what*?" Lena replied.

"I'm going to invest in the cemetery business."

CHAPTER 20—EMILY

Monday morning, Emily was tasked with the impossible. To test out if her new boss was open to courting the offer of an investment from Betsy Borden.

She left the house and walked in little zig-zags toward the funeral home, humming to herself and fidgeting her fingers between practicing conversations.

This was made all the more awkward by a rough morning for Mrs. Grimwood, who was so terribly sick that she hadn't even come down for coffee or breakfast. Norman might be late to work, in fact.

Still, Emily managed to get to the funeral home, unlock the front door and flip the open sign. She turned the lights on. Tidied Norman's desk and then her own. Watered the plants. Arranged the day's newspaper just so on the coffee table in the lobby.

Then, Emily waited.

Mr. Kreuger peeked in on her, bored, apparently. She mentioned vaguely that Mr. Grimwood would be in soon and that they had an important meeting later in the morning. The mortician already knew about this, apparently, because he nodded gravely and apologized about the meeting.

The entire conversation, however, reminded Emily just how superfluous a *second* mortuary would be. Sure, they needed more graveyard plots. But did that really necessitate a new enterprise?

She thought not.

By half past nine, Emily grew nervous. No sign of Norman and the mayor was due to arrive at ten.

After a brief contemplation, she decided to call him at the house. It felt important enough, and since Norman wasn't one to miss a meeting, she figured she'd better check to make sure things were okay.

When she called him, though, he didn't answer. The phone rang and rang, and no one picked up.

The minute hand of the old grandfather clock dragged itself to the nine. Fifteen minutes left.

Worried now, Emily thought she could run home and check on Norman and his mother. Or she could stay. Wait. And, worst case scenario, play tour guide at the cemetery.

Another five minutes of twiddling her thumbs and twirling her pencil and Emily had just one option: she'd have to stay.

Just as she stood to find Mr. Kreuger, who might be more educated on the matters of plot figures and acreage, the front door creaked open.

Emily swiveled back, fully expecting to see Norman rush in, panicked... but no.

"Mayor Brooks," she greeted, quickly plastering a smile to her mouth. "You're... *here.*"

"Yes." He grinned broadly, his arms protruding as they attempted to hang loosely along his sides. Seeing him standing there, he was nearly unrecognizable compared to the man who had sat behind a microphone and a broad, elevated cabinet.

Mayor Brooks was short. Emily's height. Five foot two. And he was as round as he was tall. "Call me Bob," he added. "Miss Emily, right?"

She was taken aback by his keen memory. It wasn't even the mayor Emily had scheduled with. It was his secretary. "Yes sir. Emily Addams. At your service." She stuck out her hand, and he took it in both of his, shaking it warmly before twisting to study the lobby.

"Haven't been in here since Mother passed." He blew a low whistle. "Hasn't changed much."

Immediately, Emily wondered if this was a bad thing. Might they lose the mayor's favor if the place wasn't up to some modern standard she didn't know about? Her mind flew into justification mode. "Oh really? Well, Mr. Grimwood is a man of tradition, you see."

"Nice plants," the mayor interjected, obviously unfazed in the least. "I don't recall there being so many."

Doubtful that he'd remember something as silly as houseplants during his own mother's funeral. Still, she humored him. "Thank you. We like to add a little life around here, of course."

Mayor Brooks laughed hard—a full-bellied laugh that reached his face, which turned red as a ripe tomato. "Good one!" he wheezed.

Emily hadn't meant it as a joke, but she smiled with him.

"Where is ol' Norm, anyway?" the man asked, peering around Emily and down the hall toward the middle of the building, where Norman's office sat.

Her heart pounded in her chest. The whole event reminded her of the time her father had come into her bedroom, where her first husband—then just a boyfriend —was hiding. Lester had crawled in through the window despite Emily's initial rejection. He had pushed his way through the half-open glass as she had tried to shoo him off, and once he was in, she could hear her father's footsteps storming down the short hall to her little bedroom. Lester had ducked beneath the bed, and once the door flew open—her father in a rage—she was caught between the two. An impossible situation. Either she confessed that her boyfriend was there before her father ripped into the room and discovered Lester for himself. Or she denied and prayed her father *wouldn't* rip into her room for once.

In the end, Emily had left the house that night. She wouldn't be back until that marriage was over and just in time for the next one to unfold. It was a wonder her father and stepmother let her come home at all. Maybe the black eye had helped them reconcile their anger with her for quartering Lester and then leaving with him, instead of staying to endure her father's wrath. She'd gotten what she deserved.

Emily swallowed and glanced at the clock again. Nearly ten now. "He's—um. Well, you see, Mayor—"

"Bob," the man interrupted. "Call me Bob!"

"Right. *Bob*. Well, there's a bit of a—well, it's Mrs. Grimwood, Norman's mother."

"Oh, right. Right." His face fell. "Sick as a dog. I heard. She drew a bum hand alright." He tilted his body just so and wriggled a half-finished cigar from one pocket, then shimmied the other way and withdrew a silver lighter.

Emily pursed her lips as he situated the thick stub in his mouth and flicked the flame into being.

She could tell the mayor the tour was cancelled and thereby compromise everything and turn the upper hand back over to Nancy. Or she could take it on herself, somehow.

Emily knew there was only one option. "That's all right, though. I can give you the tour." She smiled her winningest smile at the portly man, who beamed in response and fumbled with a gesture to the door.

"Wonderful, little lady! Just wonderful. Shall we?"

They walked together as he puffed on his cigar. It gave off a musky, perfumed aroma that Emily didn't quite mind.

She forced herself to slow down to keep tempo with Bob as he chatted about everything from the weather to how his secretary—who was technically the *Town of Gull's Landing's* secretary and not his *personal* one—was preoccupied with another matter. He fretted over how much he hated the monthly meetings where locals came to gripe and pester and how much he enjoyed the parade, which received rave reviews from the Gazette.

"Do you read the paper, Miss Emily?" he asked as they stepped through the black iron gates and onto the broad pebble path of the Second Street cemetery.

"Yes," Emily replied. "A little."

"Young people don't read the *paper* anymore. I'm glad to hear you do. It's all MTV this and stereo systems *that*. I like the movies, naturally, but the paper—now *that's* media. Oh!" he stopped short of the entryway garden bed. Emily had started clearing it of weeds and dead flowers the week before, adding fresh blooms and pruning back the centerpiece hedge before throwing down fresh straw to help ward off frost. It could have been the job of the groundsman, but Emily liked the work, so she just did it. "Lovely," Bob noted. "Reminds me of my wife's handiwork at our place."

"Is she—?" Emily began.

"Alive and well! I just mean she loves her garden. More than she loves me!" He belted out in laughter, and Emily smiled politely.

"Has she ever been a part of the local club? The gardening club, I mean?"

"Not sure," Bob replied. "She's a busy woman, what with her Canasta gals and book club and cooking society —you know women." He laughed again. "Well, of course you do, miss! You *are* one. A woman, that is."

Emily couldn't help but feel a little proud at that. She hadn't ever called herself a woman. Hadn't figured she'd earned the title quite yet. Not that she needed to hear it from a stranger or another adult, but hearing it at all— that she was a *woman*—bolstered her for what was to come: their tour.

Before they moved away from the pretty planter, Emily said, "I'm a member of the Garden Guild, that's what the gardening club goes by, you see. I'd love to invite your wife to join us. If you want to pass along our information. Or I can take hers?"

"Sure, sure. But later. I've got lunch and drinks with a general contractor after this, as a matter of fact. Big changes for Gull's Landing. A *shopping mall*. You didn't hear it from me, though!"

Emily's eyes grew wide. "A shopping mall! Where?" She couldn't fathom a good spot for a shopping mall. Not in their little hamlet on the sea.

"That's the question I intend to answer this afternoon, as you might guess. Lots of tours for Mayor Brooks today. I'll get my exercise in, no doubt!"

Emily walked on. "Right, right. Okay, well. Where do I begin?" Where *should* she begin?

"Well, you can begin by telling me where on earth— and I do mean *where* on *earth*—are the newly deceased going to fit in this place? It's beautiful, sure. The green grass. The hedges and shrubs and all the flowers—you tend it nicely, Miss Emily. You do. But it's *cramped*. See? Now look here!" He pointed with his cigar down a neat row of headstones, not a foot of space between them. And so it went on and on as they walked up and up toward the back of the property.

Emily didn't have much to add to the obvious. And if Norman had already agreed that the cemetery was nearing capacity, she wasn't quite sure *what* she ought to say.

Once they made it to the last row of headstones, Emily indicated with her hand for them to turn north, but the mayor raised a fat finger, striding across to a tree that stretched its rough branches over the back fence and into the cemetery property. He pushed the butt of his cigar into its bark and Emily watched the sizzling death of the squat thing, shuddering on behalf of the poor tree. She let out a sigh.

"If we walk this way, I can show you our most recent burial plot and the plots that are still available." She pointed again down the lane to their right.

Bob shook his head, coughing and running his hand across his forehead, smearing sweat into his tuft of slate-colored hair. "I've seen enough, and I know enough. I've got all the figures, and it's Norm who can confirm them. Not to impugn your know-how, Miss Emily," he added with a derisive chuckle and Emily started to wonder if Bob Brooks was as affable as when they'd begun. "Besides," he went on, patting his rotund middle, "a man in my shape has to rely on other people's words in this scenario, you see. I simply can't make it another step uphill. Not to say I wasn't fit as a fiddle in my younger years, mind you." He winked at Emily, and they were back on track. In a groove again as they strolled down toward the entrance.

"I can tell you that regardless of whether we do have the extra space, Bob," Emily said as they walked, "there simply isn't enough business in this town for a second mortuary."

"But surely we need a second *cemetery*, if the figures are accurate," he replied evenly.

"Yes, and I would think, sir, that Mr. Grimwood would be amenable or even *enthusiastic* about developing into the woods here or—"

"These woods are county land. He can't do that." Bob

gestured with the short butt of his defunct cigar, and the sweet, heady scent materialized again.

"In that case, maybe he has another idea," she answered. "I'm not sure."

"Sweetie," Bob cleared his throat and paused, his breath heavy. "With all due respect, the biggest reason I am even giving old Nancy Shittle—er, ShYtle or whatever —and Roy, I suppose—the time of day has nothing to do with *anything other* than this." He lifted his eyebrows at her and rubbed the tips of his fingers together.

Emily didn't know what it meant, but the gesture seemed crude.

She frowned. "Sorry, Bob. I'm not sure quite what you mean."

"I mean *money*, kid! They can develop whatever this town needs them to develop, and boy howdy *have they*! The renovated sandlot behind Barry's Dry Goods and Sundries? The Shittles. It's no sandlot anymore, kid. It's a green-as-emerald baseball field. For the kids, mind you!"

Emily winced. She had no clue the Nancy woman was a... philanthropist.

And Bob didn't stop there. "The soup kitchen on Baker? Shittles. For chrissakes, the library expansion at the south end of Elm! Shittles!" he wheezed himself into a coughing fit and tucked the cigar remnants into his pocket. "You see, Miss Emily, these folks are *good* folks. Nancy in particular. So when she comes up with a charitable idea, the mayor's job is to move out of the way. You get me?"

Emily let her shoulders sag forward as she nodded miserably.

"Listen, kid, if Norm has more to add—if he has anything... anything at *all*, you have him give me a call."

"He does." It fell out of her mouth. A fib. A secret, even. Something Mr. Grimwood didn't know about yet. Something he may not endorse. Something he may not even *pursue*. But what if she didn't say something and the mayor gave the Shytles a green light? She had to try at least. What was that expression? Better to ask forgiveness than permission?

The mayor eyed her. "Well? Out with it, kid."

"We have an investor."

CHAPTER 21—LIL

Lil was watering her spider plants in the bedroom when the doorbell chimed.

She wasn't expecting anyone, but then—that didn't mean much. Her location so close to the boardwalk meant that tourists often mistook her property for *part* of the boardwalk. A mom-and-pop shop or a quaint café, carved out of the remains of an original shoreline homestead.

It wasn't though. It was just Lil. A widow, now. No Tarot cards—the future was bright enough to give them a rest—for now, at least. She had nothing to offer anyone, really. Not even the hint of a glimpse of the woman who sat around in a saggy bathing suit all day.

Sure, she knew what people thought of her.

In a way, Lillian Gulch had turned into that gypsy from so many years ago—the one with chin whiskers and wild locks of silvery hair. Maybe that's what happened to unhappy women: they became caricatures of their former selves. Halloween costumes, even.

Lil refused to be a Halloween costume. A gypsy woman tourists would spy sitting in her bathing suit reading Tarot cards.

No, no, she wasn't going to change out of her bathing suit. Not once summer hit. And she'd still pull the cards out for fun sometimes, she would.

But there'd be more to her now. Now that Sam was out and the Garden Guild was in. And then, of course, the hopeful wisp of a new romance.

She had a lot to look forward to, Lil did.

Particularly now that winter was descending on Gull's Landing and the nights of open windows and the days of backyard sitting were creeping to an end. Some might consider cold days and bad weather and the whole of the darkest months to be just that—dark. Barren.

Not Lil, though. She saw an opportunity. A reawakening hatched before her. A chance to crawl into herself and reemerge in the following spring a new woman—not on the outside, no. But where it counted.

On the inside.

And that's how she was moving forward with her daily tasks, too.

In the days since Sam's passing, Lil had turned her attention on the house, mainly, painting the upstairs bath and vacuuming beneath the sofa cushions. Even just a single chore gave her a sense of accomplishment, and she'd celebrate every thing—even just making the bed—with fifteen minutes of a crossword or an episode of one her favorite daytime soaps.

That day, upstairs in the master bedroom, as she studied the stream of water bubbling into the soil of the green-leafed plants, she thought about how odd life would be without other people in it. What if she hadn't warmed to Betsy Borden? What if Emily Addams had never moved to town? What might've become of Lil then?

Though she wasn't expecting company, she *was* expecting to hear from Emily soon.

The girl had promised them that she would deliver the good news of Betsy's offer to Norman. Emily had also promised that after she told Norman about it, she'd make the rounds on the phone. Lil was dying to know how it all went. If there was a future alliance for the Garden Guild and Second Street Mortuary. Good thing Lil had joined. Had she not, the other two might have barreled ahead without her.

Norman might have slipped right through her fingers. Another man lost to the sands of time and the tragedies of one poor choice.

The doorbell rang again, stirring Lil back to the present.

She set the watering can down and made her way to the first floor and the foyer, reaching for the knob and opening the door to a pleasant surprise.

"Lil." A broad smile crept across Norman Grimwood's face as he stood, alone, on her front stoop. A limp bouquet of sunflowers in his hand. "How do you do?"

She grinned at his formality and his awkward presence and presentation, in jeans and a sweater with the yellow flowers and the old-fashioned greeting.

"Norman, hello. Do come in." She waved him into the house and stepped aside, her hand on the doorknob, palm slick with sweat, heart racing in her chest. Desire churning in her stomach as his cologne made its way to her, heady and masculine. A stark contrast to his usual softness.

"It's been a day," he started without prompting. "Quite a day."

Lil showed him to the kitchen, where he passed the flowers to her and she accepted them, searching beneath the kitchen sink for a crystal vase and filling it with water as he stood at the table, his hands working nervously into his pockets.

She turned with the flowers in the vase, the arrangement heavier now that its stalks steeped in water. "These are lovely. Thank you. Can I get you coffee? Tea? Something stronger?"

He licked his lips and shook his head. "No, no. I only stopped by briefly. To give you these and thank you. You and the others."

After setting the flowers on a cream lace doily in the center of the table, she folded her hands in front of her. "All right. But, what for?"

"It's just been a day, really. You see my mother, she's... she's sick. She had a bad spell this morning, and I took her to the hospital."

"Is she all right?" Lil's eyebrows crumpled together high on her head. Worry trilled in her voice and though she didn't know Norman's mother, she saw their close bond. Knew the pain of death... or sickness. Knew how crushing a feeling it was to watch someone you loved struggle. She'd seen it with her brother.

Sam, too, but he—well...

"She's better now. Much better. We've got her on

home rest. Palliative. She's comfortable, and she's okay." His eyes watered, and Lil's own throat constricted for the poor man.

"You should be with her," Lil pointed out, suddenly awkward feeling that his mother was so close to death at home—just out of a morning in the hospital—and here he was, bringing *Lil* flowers.

"Oh, Lil," he dropped his head into his hands, and they shook. Oh, did they shake, and Lil saw his crushing pain and it was all she could do not to cross to him and wrap her arms around this sweet man—a man who loved his mother, who brought women flowers and who hired poor young girls and gave peace to families in their hardest times.

She swallowed. "Norman, what can I do?"

"You've done quite a lot. Betsy, Lena, Emily. And you. All of you. That's why I'm here. I, um, I went to Betsy's house first, but she redirected me, you see."

Frowning, Lil answered. "What do you mean?"

"Her investment. Emily told me about Betsy Borden's offer to help fund an expansion. You see—" he blinked away the wetness in his eyes and ran the backs of his hands across his cheeks as he regained his balance. "When she told me, we called Betsy right off. Apparently, Bob Brooks had already come by for the tour, but Emily walked him around and indicated we might have a way to offer more plots. He took her word for it, and then when I returned to the funeral home from the hospital, she told me all about it. We called Betsy together, Betsy confirmed, and I accepted. Without that—I don't know what I'd do, Lil. If the Shytles open a second cemetery, it'd cause a strain. It would. Burials make up a significant proportion of our revenue, if you can believe that. I would *hate* to raise coffin prices. Then again, maybe Nancy would allow me to continue providing the burial services, but we'd have to pay her fee, I'd think. It could be a mess. It really could. And what if she decides she likes it? And she wants to open a mortuary to go with the cemetery? Lil, Betsy's investment might save Second Street."

"You were never going to lose your business, Norman," Lil offered, confused at what he said. "Right? I mean, surely Nancy—despite it all—was only going to open a second burial ground. You could still reap the burial costs."

He shook his head. "No, you're right. But don't you *know* Nancy Shytle and her husband? Roy? They *own* this town, Lil. If they decide to buy something... to *sell* something—it's theirs. And if they want a piece of the mortuary business—even if it's just a cemetery... that was never going to end well for me. But I had no way to respond. Nothing to offer."

Lil smiled and clasped her hands by her face, about to reply, but he went on.

"But the thing of it is, Lil—" his smile slipped away.

She blinked. "Yes?"

Lil watched as Norman's Adam's apple bobbed up and down and he ran his tongue over his lips, his eyebrows falling lower over his eyes. "Why?"

There was no easy answer to his question. No explaining to a strange man why four strange women were so dead set on rushing to his aid.

This was exactly how Lil replied at first.

"It's complicated," she answered. "Women are complicated, I suppose." Her brows knit together, and she worried a hangnail with her teeth.

"Can you explain it to me? I can't—" his voice dropped lower. "Lil, I can't commit to bringing Betsy into the business if I don't have the full picture. Why do you want to help me? All of you?"

"It's a long story." Lil didn't mean to say that. It wasn't really a long story. It was just—it was just that there was a lot to say, and Lil thought of poor old Irma laid up in bed, sick with cancer. "I know you have to go."

He nodded. "I do."

An uncomfortable silence fell between them before he frowned and turned toward the door. "Maybe you can explain another time."

"Of course. Yes. In the meantime, you should take the money. Take the money and make a plan. Norman, don't let Nancy win."

"It's not a competition, Lil," he reasoned as they moved to the front door together. "Is it?"

She didn't answer at first, blinking instead. "Not exactly. Not for *you*. It's—like I said, Norman. It's a conversation for another time."

"How about Friday night? Seven o'clock at Maeve's? I can pick you up."

Lil pressed her hand to her chest. "Oh my," she breathed.

"What do you say, Lil?" Norman looked bashful. Adorably so.

And still, all she could answer with was, "I'm not sure."

CHAPTER 22—BETSY

"Friday? That's the day after Thanksgiving," Betsy pointed out at Bingo. She'd accepted that having new friends meant allowing Bingo to play second fiddle for once.

Lil busied herself with her mug of hot cocoa, stirring the marshmallows into oblivion. "I wasn't going to go anyway," she muttered.

"No, no, no," Betsy protested. "You should definitely go out with him, Lil. I was thinking out loud. Ma and I usually do Thanksgiving here, at the club. What are you doing this year?" Betsy stared hard at Lil. It ought to have occurred to her to check in sooner. Then again, she knew Lil had family in Philadelphia. "Are you going back home to Philly?"

Lil shrugged. "I was going to, sure. But then Norm stopped by and—"

"Norm?" Lena lifted an eyebrow and pointed a finger at Lil. "Sounds like you have all the reason in the world to stick around town. Norm." She chuckled to herself.

Betsy lifted an eyebrow at the cackling old woman. "Ignore her, Lil. Although, I'll admit, she makes a good point, but listen, if you are staying, why not join us here?"

Lil lowered her head, drew the mug to her lips, and took a slow sip. When she ducked down, Betsy spotted Bill at the table beyond. They locked eyes, briefly, and Betsy shivered. Every hour that stretched on in her life, she thought about the obnoxious stranger even more. Questions percolated in her mind. How long had he lived in Gull's Landing? Where was he from? Why did he move to The Landing? Why was he such fast friends with Greg Rosen?

Before Lil straightened, Bill smiled at Betsy. A crooked, awkward smile. A chink in the armor of his flashy, handsome exterior. The side of his upper lip hung high on his left canine tooth, sticking there as his smile fell away and rendering him an inadvertent goofball for a moment.

Betsy couldn't help it. She snorted a laugh, and the poor, goofy jerk flushed bright red, shook his head back at her, smiled again and shrugged.

And just like that, Betsy was interested.

"What about you, Emily?" her mother interrupted the moment, dragging Betsy's attention off of Bill.

"Hm?" Emily replied, her mouth full of popcorn.

"Thanksgiving? Are you going back to Wildwood? Your dad and stepmother are there, right?"

Emily folded her lips between her teeth and winced.

"You okay?" Betsy asked her, glancing once more to Bill, who'd twisted away and chatted with someone from the table behind him.

"It's just—Mrs. Grimwood. She can't cook right now, and I'd hate to leave them—her and Norman, I mean."

"Maybe you should stay," Lil pointed out. "Would your folks mind very much?"

Emily's face turned pale, and her eyes crinkled at the edges. "I have no idea. I haven't been good about calling."

"Have they called you?" Betsy asked pointedly. She sensed that things were tense at the Addams home front, even though Emily had kept fairly mum about it.

The young girl shook her head. "It's... complicated."

The host tapped the microphone, and Betsy's head swiveled to him.

"Never mind," Emily murmured.

Betsy hadn't gotten her two new game cards yet. None of them were prepared for the second round. They'd spent too much time chatting. Staring at attractive men. At least, Betsy had.

She muttered a swear, looked at Emily, then made a quick decision. "Screw the next round. Let's just—let's talk."

Wetness appeared on Emily's cheeks—anyway, that's what Betsy thought she saw. But the girl rubbed it quickly away.

Lil and Lena, who downed the last of their drinks and eyed the bar, had missed the moment. All of it.

"Complicated, huh?" Betsy said to Emily as she threw a sidelong glance to her mother and a meaningful eyebrow lift to Lil. "Complicated is interesting."

Emily shrank into herself, clearly unsure how to respond.

Betsy treaded lightly. "Life is complicated no matter who you are or where you come from." She ran her tongue over her lips and took a swig of her drink. "Take my father, for example," she went on, easing back into her seat as she thumbed her mug. "John Borden. Town legend, really. He was the sort who knew everyone. And everyone knew him. They still do. Great guy. Lotta dough. Lotta success. Beautiful wife—" Betsy lifted a hand to Lena who preened at the compliment. "Beautiful kid—" Betsy indicated herself and laughed too loudly. Beyond Emily and Lil, Bill peered her way. Her smile drifted to him, but she lowered her voice. "Listen, Emily. I joke, really, I do. About the beautiful stuff—"

"Hey!" Lena cried.

"Ma, come on. We're each beautiful in our own way. Right? Anyway, Emily," Betsy laid her hand on the space of table in front of Emily. "My dad was good at work. He was good with people—customers, at least. Colleagues. Competitors, even. And he provided for us. Plain as day, you can see that. But he was no father. Not in the full sense of the word." Betsy could sense her mother's feathers ruffling, but she didn't care. "He was a supervisor. A business mentor, sure. But he never kissed me goodnight. He never hugged me or tickled me until I couldn't breathe or made me a sloppy peanut butter sandwich with too much jelly and the crusts still on it."

"Neither did mine," Emily managed meekly.

"And your mother? What about your mother?" Lena prodded. Betsy kicked her gently beneath the table. Too much. Too soon. Too fast. The woman had no feel for timing. No couth, either.

But surprising to all of them, Emily replied easily. "She left when I was little. I don't know where she went."

Betsy nodded, her brows falling low over her eyes. "That's rough, huh?"

Emily shrugged. "Life goes on. Life went on."

"Your dad remarried," Lil said as a matter of fact. A piece of evidence to validate Emily's measurement of her parental experience.

Emily nodded.

"And you—" Betsy went on, "You've been married, too?"

"What?" Lena gasped.

Betsy rolled her eyes. "Ma, get with the program."

"How did you know?" Emily asked, bewildered and panicked.

Betsy covered the girl's hand in hers. "There's a difference," she replied warmly, "between a scared twenty-year-old girl and a scrappy twenty-year-old woman. You don't get scrappy just by moving to a new town. It takes a scrappy person to move to begin with. Mark my words. I'm not very scrappy. And anyway, you have that air about you. Someone who's lived a thousand lives. Someone who's loved a man. Who was with a man in every sense of the word. As much as a woman can be with a man, you were. I can see it in you, Emily Addams. You've been married."

A smirk crept across Emily's mouth. "Twice."

"Huh?" Lena made a show of tugging her ear and twisting her neck so she could hear Emily better.

Lil exchanged a look with Betsy who cocked her head. "Twice what?"

"Married twice."

Betsy's jaw hit the table.

"Wait a minute," Lena interjected, her face pulling down hard, her skin settling into the folds along her neck. "You've been married twice? And you're *twenty*? You're twenty-years-old and twice married?"

Emily offered a sad smile in return and nodded. "Yeah."

Lil spoke next. "I get it."

"Huh?" Betsy cried, unable to hold back. It was a shock. It was one thing to be married once by twenty. But... twice? Then it occurred to her. "Oh. Widowed, I bet."

But Emily shook her head miserably.

"What, are you a polygamist? I hear those exist, you know."

"What's that?" Emily asked, bewildered, evidently.

Betsy explained, "You know, a polygamist. A... a swinger, I guess. Married to two or more men at the same time. Although I think it's more typically a man married to two or more women at the same time. It's an old-timey thing. Think along the lines of Abraham and Sarah. Biblical stuff."

Emily giggled, and it served to break the shock and tension that had gripped them. "Two failed marriages. Different ones."

"Sheesh," Betsy answered. "You got me beat twice over."

"Is that a good thing or a bad thing?" Lena asked.

"I'd call it a good thing. I mean, marriage is the goal, right? So, to do it twice, well... that means you've got two more men than I have who want to marry you. And, if my math is correct, twice as many men as ol' Lena, here, too." Betsy laughed, but Lena rolled her eyes.

"Just because you marry a man, doesn't mean he loves you," Emily murmured.

Betsy softened. "That's probably true."

"And so is the reverse," her mother pointed out. "Just because you don't marry a man doesn't mean he doesn't love you."

Betsy cocked her head to her mother, about to ask her a follow-up to that little gem.

But Lil beat her to the punch. "Sometimes, marriage is the worst thing in the world."

The other three all turned their gazes on Lil.

"What?" The sound of the host calling out numbers, the presence of Bill-the-Neighbor in the backdrop, the yearning for a second mug of hot cocoa—it all fell away as Betsy asked the question, her tone flat.

Lil's eyes dropped to her own mug, marshmallow residue peeking from the inner rim. She looked up but turned to Emily, ignoring Betsy's question. "It's impressive, Emily."

"Impressive?" Emily flicked a nervous glance to Betsy, who also didn't know where Lil was heading.

Lena did, apparently, because she answered for all of them, her words directed at Emily. "It's impressive that you managed to get out of two marriages, much less one."

"You loved Dad," Betsy pointed out. "What are you talking about?"

Lena clicked her tongue. "Never mind."

"She's right," Lil replied. "Leaving a marriage isn't easy. How'd you manage that, Emily?"

Betsy was lost. Totally lost. Here she was, a grown woman on the downward slope, years older than Emily and years wiser, too. And yet the three of them were speaking a different language. Married language. Or... formerly married, as the case may be.

"The first, my father had annulled. The second— well... technically, we're still married. I filed, though," she rushed to add. "It's just a matter of him signing and so forth."

"So, you're not divorced, then?" Betsy asked, more confused than ever.

"Not yet," Emily admitted. "But I will be. I'm sure."

"Can I ask you why?" Betsy softened her tone.

Emily's chest rose and fell and she swallowed visibly. "Well, the first one—Mark—he broke my nose." She tapped the bridge, and Betsy spied, for the first time, a crook.

"Oh, my word," Lena gasped. "Oh, my word."

Emily shrugged. "It was easy to get the annulment. The second, well, I thought he was—he just... he just... he wasn't nice?" It came out like a question.

"You thought he might do the same thing as the first," Betsy offered.

Emily nodded. "I got a little scared. But not too scared. Not too scared to, you know, get out of it. To send him the paperwork."

Betsy looked at Lil then at her mother. "Am I the only one, then?"

"The only what?" Lena asked.

"The only one who hasn't had a bum marriage?"

"You're the only one who hasn't had a marriage at all," Lena replied. "So, yes, I suppose you are the only one."

"You and Dad? You had a bad marriage?" It was like the world was crumbling around her. Betsy had lived all her life under the natural assumption that they were happy. All of them. Especially Lena and John.

"It wasn't a bad marriage, no. But you said it yourself, Bets. John was a supervisor. More of a supervisor than a husband or a father." She looked thoughtful, or as thoughtful as Betsy had ever seen her mother look.

"So you didn't love him?"

"I loved him as much as a wife loves a husband, sure."

"I loved Lester. And Jimmy, too," Emily chimed in. "But that was the problem."

"And you, Lil? Sam?" Betsy looked at Lil whose face was stone. "Word has it that Sam Gulch was a sweet guy. A doll. Everyone loved him!"

"Yeah," Lil answered, her mouth a scowl. "That was the problem."

CHAPTER 23—EMILY

With some deal of trepidation, Emily ended up asking Mr. Grimwood if she might invite a friend to Thanksgiving.

Having worded it exactly like that, he immediately said no. "Let's keep it to family," he'd replied softly.

Family.

Emily had lived with Norman and Irma for just over a month. Surely, they didn't consider her family. Not yet at least.

But she'd take it. She'd take whatever she could get. Particularly since she'd told her father she would not be returning home for Thanksgiving and he'd told her that, in that case, she wasn't invited back for Christmas.

Emily had turned as red as a cranberry when Norman both rejected her and offered his affections in one fell swoop, and she apologized but also mentioned that it was only Lil Gulch.

At that, Norman had changed his tune.

"If it's not a gentleman friend, then of course she's welcome."

Irma, who'd been feeling well enough to sit in the living room during the conversation, intervened just then. "Emily can invite whomever she'd like. This is Thanksgiving, after all, Norman."

He'd winced and readily agreed. "Invite who you wish, Emily. You've worked hard. You deserve it."

But it wasn't Emily who went ham with the invitations.

ON THURSDAY OF THAT WEEK, Betsy and Lena were first to arrive at the Grimwoods', their arms weighed down with heavy casserole dishes.

Emily looked beyond them to see Lil parking her car, too. "Oh," she said, glancing behind her. "I wondered who Irma was talking to," Emily said, smiling at the women.

"Lena invited herself, and therefore me," Betsy replied. "But Irma wouldn't have it any other way. At least, that's what she said on the phone."

"You invited yourself?" Emily asked Lena. She took the hot dish, a towel wrapped around it, before stepping back into the house.

"I called Irma and asked if she'd come to the club, but you were right," Lena said, her voice low, as she unraveled a scarf from her neck. "She wants to stay here. So, I figured it wouldn't hurt if she had more company. Low numbers around the holidays can really bring out the depression in people. And that's if you *don't* have terminal cancer."

"Ma," Betsy hissed.

"Hi Lil!" Emily called over the two of them, excited now that the whole of the Garden Guild was in attendance. It'd make things all the more comfortable. She just hoped the turkey didn't run out.

Especially when she saw a red BMW pull up behind Lil's on the street.

"Is that?" she hooked a finger to the car.

Betsy grabbed it and tugged her inside. "Yep."

AFTER THE CLATTER of getting the table set and a drawn-out grace, courtesy of Lena, they settled into a contented chatter.

The turkey, it turned out, would have gone to waste had the extra visitors not appeared.

"I tell you what, whoever's working the dining room at the club is going to have a lot of extra time on his hands. Look at us—half the neighborhood is at Norman Grimwood's, for Pete's sake," Lena huffed.

"I assure you they'll have more than enough diners," Bill pointed out.

Emily saw Betsy smirk at him, but behind the smirk was a small smile.

Emily lifted an eyebrow and stabbed at a particularly juicy chunk of meat. "Does anyone here know Mr. Brooks' wife?" she said, testing the waters of introducing a new member to the club.

Soon, it'd be December, and after that January, and they had the long stretch of winter to make it as a group. They needed tasks, sure, but they needed people, too. People with ideas for the Garden Guild. People to help prepare for the Saturday farmers' markets and the harvest festival the following summer and fall. Emily was in full-on planning mode. She had to be.

Because Jimmy refused to sign the divorce papers.

If Emily didn't have a clear something to pin her to Gull's Landing—something more than a secretary gig—then how could she convince a judge that the marriage could be over? That she didn't need him? She didn't need alimony. She didn't need a marriage. She just needed the dang divorce.

"Glenda?" Norman asked. "Sure, I do. Bob's wife."

Irma coughed into her fist, and all eyes fell to the center of the table, as if to try and ignore the obvious.

Emily lowered her voice. "You okay, Irma?"

"Yes," she managed, through a second fit. "I, um. I know Glenda, too." She cleared her throat and took a long, slow sip of her water.

"You do?" Norman asked.

"Sure, I do. Her father worked with yours." A motherly smile lifted the woman's wan cheeks, and Emily wanted to rest her hand against the woman's skin. To cradle her and be cradled by her.

It was no wonder Norman was still so close to Irma. She was the single kindest woman Emily had ever met in her entire life.

Lena cleared her throat at the other end of the table. "What did he do again? Your husband, Irma?"

"Earl. Earl was his name, and he worked on the north dock—the one near the Pier." She coughed into her napkin.

Norman reached across to her and rested a hand on her shoulder. "He got caught in a storm when I was just a kid. Whole vessel drowned."

"That's right." Irma had recovered, but Emily couldn't help but notice the dark red stain in her napkin. Her stomach churned. "What do you want with Glenda, Emily?"

"Well, she loves to garden. I thought we could reach out to her. Invite her to join the club."

"It's winter," Lena pointed out. "Nothing for us to do. Wait until spring, and we'll get back to it."

"I think it's great that Emily is dedicated. We could talk to Glenda if you'd like, Em," Lil replied, offering a warm smile.

"Speaking of the Garden Guild," Betsy interjected, dabbing her red lips with her napkin. Emily felt sad as she considered the stark contrast between boisterous Betsy and poor, sweet Irma.

But there was no time for that, because the woman launched directly into a dominating review of her financial plans for the mortuary.

"I'm not sure everyone here is aware," her eyes seemed to linger on Bill, which Emily noticed with care. "But," Betsy went on, "I'll be financially investing in our very own local mortuary and cemetery business. Second Street. Norm and I will be business partners, and what's more, the Garden Guild will officially sponsor a monument on the new site."

"A new site?" Greg chimed in. "Lena didn't mention a new site."

Lena scowled at him. "That's because we don't talk, Greg."

Emily glanced from Betsy to Lena to Lil, the last of whom shrugged. "I didn't know the four of you were so well-acquainted at all," Lil pointed out as she slipped a spoonful of stuffing into her mouth.

"We aren't," Betsy huffed.

"Then how—?" Emily started, but Mr. Grimwood cut her off.

"I invited Bill. He asked to bring Greg Rosen, here, and well, Mother was okay with it—she likes a big to-do, you see. We don't have many big to-dos. Not around here, at least."

"Oh?"

"Norm and I go way back. My dad handled his dad's estate. Cohen Family Law Firm in Ocean City, ever heard of it? That was my dad. I've moved our offices here, though. Wanted a slower pace. Somewhere with less traffic."

"Oh," Betsy replied through a mouthful of food.

"We handle estate planning, and Earl Grimwood hadn't done a lick of that, you see."

Emily glanced awkwardly at Norman, who appeared unfazed.

"When my dad passed, we were destitute. Mother tried to recover wages due to him as well as a modest penchant, but there was nothing. She reached out to Mr. Cohen back then to see about insurance, and he helped us get back on our feet. He helped Mother get hired on here, in fact. She took on a side job as a seamstress in this house, here, which was the original Gull's Landing Mortuary. She worked upstairs, where I did my studies in the evenings. Eventually, I came to learn the business and took over. That's basically it."

"What do you mean you came to learn the business and took over? Sewing?" Betsy asked, rapt.

Norman laughed. "Oh, no. I mean the mortuary business. You see—I became... entranced, I suppose. The man who ran it, he hired me on to do grunt work, and—well, you see, my father—he never had a proper burial."

Emily studied her boss hard, seeing him in a new light. Seeing him for the first time. She'd never thought to ask how he had gotten started in his business. She had never given the business much thought to begin with.

"You mean your father isn't buried in Second Street?" Betsy asked earnestly.

"Oh, no. He's somewhere in the Atlantic Ocean. I don't have a single relation in Second Street."

Irma added, "My family is from Newark. Earl had no one. No one at all."

"Well, I know what that's like," Lena added usefully.

All heads turned to her. "John is in Milwaukee. We didn't even go to the service."

Emily gasped. "You didn't go to your husband's funeral?"

But she just shook her head as Betsy shrugged.

"He wanted to be with his family. I wanted to stay here, with mine." Lena licked the back of her spoon before plunging into her cranberry sauce again. "There's more to it, but that's all I'll get into with mixed company."

Lena lowered her eyes and Emily marveled at the woman's transformation only long enough for Greg to break the silence.

"Lena's family is in Second Street," he offered.

Emily watched as Lena threw him a sharp glare, but she recovered quickly and nodded. "Yes. That's right."

"You don't have a plot there, though, right, Mrs. Borden?" Norman asked. "For yourself? Betsy?" Emily noted that Norman knew this sort of information. If Emily ever owned her own cemetery, she'd see to it that she would know, too.

She shook her head. "No, no. No plot. When the time comes, I'll go wherever they put me."

Emily jumped into the conversation. "Is it true the woods out back of the cemetery are county land?"

Norman looked at her and blinked dully. "I'd imagine so. Why?"

"I was wondering where we could expand to. You know, when it comes time."

"I'm not sure that we can expand at all," Norman confessed. "I don't own any other land."

"But you have me," Betsy pointed out. "We just have to find a lot. Together."

Norman let out a breath. "If we are going to insist that Nancy doesn't build a new cemetery from the ground up, then we can't build one that way either."

"Maybe we can find a different place. Somewhere that isn't in the middle of town," Betsy offered.

Lil's eyes flashed up and she gripped the table on either side of her, her hand inches from Emily's. "I might have something in mind."

CHAPTER 24—LIL

Thanksgiving was as eventful a holiday as Lil had ever been to. Even as a child, when her parents would gather cousins and uncles and aunts around the table in their downtown Philly apartment, it didn't feel as full as it had at Norman's.

They'd ended the night with a toast and easy good-byes at the front door. Lil promised both Betsy and Norman that she'd do a little groundwork on her locale idea. Only then was Lil willing to come out with it. She didn't want to get anyone's hopes up too high, after all.

THE VERY NEXT MORNING, she'd finished her groundwork. But instead of placing a simple call to Norman, she decided to drive to him. After all, she was just down the road.

Emily answered the door a tad confused. "Lil?"

"Emily, hi. I, um, came to tell Norman that Betsy won't be along to get her car. At least, not until later."

"Lil." Her name came from somewhere behind Emily, down a darkened hall.

She looked past the girl to meet Norman's gaze. He wore a tidy maroon sweater and relaxed khaki pants. Hair combed neatly. Eyeglasses sitting on his nose with a folded newspaper in one hand.

"Hi Norman, I just came by to tell you that Betsy will come for her car later."

"And the place," he added, taking Emily's spot by the door as Emily drifted away.

"Pardon?" Lil asked, her heart pounding in her chest. Even the sight of Norman was enough to fill her hollow chest with butterflies. Ridiculous, really.

"Last night, you said you'd take me to the place you had in mind. For the expansion?"

She knew what he meant. Of course, she did.

That very morning, she had arrived at St. Gert's first thing. On her way to Betsy's, she had swung into the little parish rectory and knocked gently, asking the secretary within about the weedy, wooded parcel that stretched as far as the eye could see down behind the church. And the news wasn't good.

"Right," she replied, chewing her lower lip. "Actually, I'm not sure about that after all."

"Oh." Norman's face fell, then he glanced behind himself and down the hall. When he looked back at her, Lil's pulse had steadied.

"I can still show you, though, if you want?"

A grin formed across his mouth. "I'd like that," he said. "I'd like that very much."

NORMAN DROVE them in his black town car, which people likely mistook for a hearse. It wasn't a hearse. But when the funeral director drives a sleek, chrome-trimmed, black town car, well, it comes across a lot like a hearse.

She directed him to St. Gertrude's, tugging her sweater around her chest for warmth and to hide the rise and fall of her breaths in such close proximity to him.

"About tonight," Norman started as they turned onto Finch Street.

Lil blinked. She'd told him no. Just after Thanksgiving dinner, while everyone else had tucked into the living room with a drink in hand. It was a soft *no*. An apologetic one. One filled with regret and disappointment and fear.

But she had said no.

Now, she licked her lips, prepared to take it back. To tell him *yes* instead of no. To explain herself.

"I'm really sorry, Lil." He frowned at her. "I shouldn't have put you on the spot like that. You must think I'm a real creep."

"Oh!" Lil replied, her voice shrill and uneven. "*No*. No, no. Norman, not at all. I was—I *am* flattered. And... I would like to go to dinner with you. Truly, I would. It's just—"

"Sam," he answered heavily. "I'm a terrible cad. How could I put you in that position?"

She left it at that, worrying her lower lip as he parked in front of the rectory.

"It's just this way." Lil led the way, walking ahead of Norman down the little path that spilled out to the hidden, brushy field of headstones.

Once they'd made it to the field, she turned. "See?"

He squinted and took a step forward, hesitant and tender-footed as he studied the sun-washed, moss-eaten stones. "I've never been down here," he confessed. "I didn't even *know* about this place. Have you asked the church?"

She nodded enthusiastically. "The secretary didn't know much other than that it's owned by St. Gertrude's. She said it's defunct. They don't use it anymore. They haven't used it since she's been around, and she doesn't know much more."

Norman walked further down the row, stopping ahead at the next stone, yards off. "There aren't many, are there?"

"Many?" she asked.

"There aren't many graves here for such a vast property." He straightened and held a hand out to indicate the distance. "Look how far it goes. All the way into the woods to that fence back there, I'd imagine. Or am I wrong?"

Lil shrugged. "I'm not sure."

"And that way? How far that way does it span?" he pointed north toward the road that intersected Finch Street.

Again, Lil lifted her shoulders. This time, she folded

her arms across her chest to shield against a bitter breeze. "I'm not sure. I haven't walked it."

"Incredible," Norman breathed.

Lil's spirit lifted at his compliment. "It could work?"

"Well, I'm not sure. I mean, if the church owns it— we'd have to *purchase* it."

"That's what Betsy's for," Lil pointed out.

"Right, but... she can only buy it—*we* can only buy it if the church is willing to *sell* it."

"True." Lil joined him in front of a particularly plain headstone. The name read John Doe. The dates: *Unknown—1939*.

"And you never knew about this place? Not when you were a kid?"

He shook his head.

"What about the previous funeral home owner? Did they mention it?"

"Second Street was already established when I came on," he answered. "So, no. I don't recall ever knowing about it, I'm a little embarrassed to admit."

"Look," Lil pointed west to another craggy stone. "Another John Doe. That's odd."

"Oh my *word*," Norman gasped. "This isn't a normal cemetery."

Lil took a step back, steeling herself against his words. "What do you *mean* it's not a *normal* cemetery?"

Norman stepped back, too, nearly tripping over a hidden, shrunken, *wooden* marker—another nameless, half-dated inscription nearly faded into the sands of time.

"It's a potter's field."

"What's a *potter's* field?" Lil recoiled from him, a little scared, now. Another blustering wind blew down the gully. A tremble coursed through her body and Norman took notice.

He gripped her shoulders and rubbed them, warming her. "I have an extra coat, if you need one?"

She shook her head. All Lil wanted was to know if her idea was a good one. If they could expand there, in the unusual cemetery. "A potter's field?" she asked again. "What, is it—a place where artisans are buried or something? Or clergy? Like a... a dedicated memorial ground, like Arlington National Cemetery or something?"

He shook his head. "Dedicated, yes. But not for artisans or clergy. Potter's fields are for indigents. Used to be for criminals, too. Still are. Anyone society throws away, they're laid to rest in a potter's field."

Lil curled her body into Norman, who wrapped his arm around her shoulders, tugging her close. She kept her gratitude silent as her pulse fluttered back to life. "So all of these graves—they're... they're vagabonds? Outcasts?"

"Mhm," Norman's reply reverberated through her body and Lil shuddered once more.

"Come on," he said. "Let's get you back to the car."

If only she could confess that it wasn't the cold that was making her shake. It was the *heat*.

"Don't you want to walk the property? See if you could use it?"

He squeezed her deeper into him. "We have to ask the church if they'd sell. That's the first step. Then we can ask about the acreage and *then* we can conduct a review."

"What would you do if you *did* use it?" she asked as

they returned to the car, picking their way through the soggy earth and back up the hill to the parking lot. "Can you... excavate what's here? Start over? Or bury around the current graves?"

"You can excavate, yes. But I would never do that. It's unethical, in my book. Unkind, too. Regardless of who rests here, they don't deserve that. No one does."

Nancy Shytle came to mind, but Lil kept her opinion to herself. "The secretary should still be in. Let's go find out if the church might like to make a sale."

CHAPTER 25—LIL

In fact, St. Gertrude's was very keen to make money. The land was no good to them just sitting there, unbuildable and sacred. Ideally, someone *would* come along and offer to buy it, the priest had told them.

Lil didn't ask why they hadn't simply put it on the market, but then—the answer was fairly clear. Any church willing to sell off the graves of the poorest folks in town probably wasn't a church a lost soul might flock to.

After they discussed a price and took a second foot tour of the property, it became clearer and clearer that Lil's idea *was* a good one. A very good one.

"This whole lot out here," Father Bart waved his hand at the outer edge of the embankment, "is clear. They saved it in case they needed more use. This was back before Second Street Cemetery was built, of course."

Norman nodded. "In the county, we rotate now."

"Rotate?" Lil asked.

"That's right. We take turns, I guess you could say, preparing and burying those with no family. Those who die in the night in the streets. In prison. The very sick, too. Homeless. We take turns and write it off as a loss." He winced. "Crude, I know."

"You could fit at least two thousand souls on those far acres, and that doesn't account for the extra space on these two here."

"Four acres in total?" Norman whistled. "And you're certain you wish to sell?"

"Like I said, there isn't much we wish to do with the land. For the right price, we can make this happen. And we can work together, naturally. It'll serve us both well."

"Have the Shytles, by chance, contacted you about their idea to erect a second cemetery?" Lil asked out of curiosity.

The priest shook his head. "No, no. Not familiar with them. You're it."

"We can call our investor now. Get the ball rolling, if you're serious, Father Bart," Norman offered.

Lil watched the older man's eyes, gray and tired. He furrowed his brow and gave a short, assured nod. "Serious as a heart attack. I'll call the Bishop. You call your investor. We'll get it started."

WHEN THEY LEFT—AFTER Betsy gave the greenlight over the phone and the Bishop agreed to sign off, too—a thought occurred to Lil. Something that might change the proceedings.

"Norman," she said, the air from the vents finally

turning warm as they coasted down Finch Street. "What about the mayor? And Nancy?"

"What?" he asked. "You don't think he'll approve this?"

She thought for a moment. "There's no reason he shouldn't. It's just…"

"Just what, Lil?" Norman gave her a soft look, his puppy-dog eyes tilting toward her, melting her and reminding her what a stupid thing it was to say no to a date with Norm. It wasn't the 1800s. Surely a widow didn't have to wait a full calendar year to turn her blood back on.

"Can we take a detour?"

His eyes widened behind his glasses. "A detour? Is it another hidden cemetery?" A wide smile cracked across his face, drawing lines around his mouth and eyes and making him adorably irresistible to Lil.

"I've got the leftovers I took home last night, a bottle of wine, and a half-eaten cheesecake. Store bought. Interested?" She gave him a crooked smile of her own, and somehow—it worked.

"Sounds divine," he replied, turning onto Boardwalk Boulevard and down toward Lil's beachfront cottage. Just Lil's now.

Not Sam's.

Not anymore.

Not ever again.

Once they arrived, Lil started to let herself out of the car—but not before Norman dashed around and opened the door for her, taking her hand as if they were, after all, on a date.

Lil hoped they were.

Anyway, whatever it was, they were in a private place. A place hidden from the prying eyes of the rest of the town.

"I'll take your coat," she said as he followed her in through the door.

He shook it off—a heavy, dark, waterproof thing—practical but somehow elegant. She hung it in the hall closet with hers and gestured to the kitchen. "Shall we?"

Norman clasped his hands behind his back and nodded shyly. "I'll follow your lead."

It was perhaps the first time Lil had ever heard that from a man. She hadn't normally been much of a leader when it came to romance.

Then it occurred to her that this—*this* with Norman—it wasn't romance. It was... business. The cemetery. The funeral home. The future. Nancy. *Business.*

So then why was she about to tell Norman what had happened? Why was she about to confess the sins of the past to him if it wasn't personal? If it was just... business?

CHAPTER 26—BETSY

With December in full swing, Christmas shopping was well underway. Betsy had quite a list this year. And no longer was she searching for something generic she could buy in bulk and distribute like a delivery person. Without the office staff of Book with Borden in her life—and without Nancy or Pam to shop for—she could actually have fun for once. No more tins of danish cookies and gift cards to the safest bet in town.

She got to pick out nice things. Personal things. Not just for Lena and Lil and Emily, either. Norman and Irma Grimwood had also made the cut. And so, too, had Greg and Bill. Reluctant though Betsy was to admit it, tensions were cooling between the foursome. Would-be foursome, rather. In fact, tensions were cooling so much that a warmness had taken place of the stilted relationships.

It all started on the first of December, when Betsy had arrived at the clubhouse after signing off on the sale of what they now called Finch Street Cemetery. That name might change—they might form a coalition of cemeteries or perhaps dub it Borden Boneyard (although, Betsy hadn't made ins with that moniker quite yet; too brash, apparently).

She had just popped in for a hot tea—something to warm her up after a brisk walk through the new property. Coincidentally, Bill was there, too. Without Greg, for once.

It gave her an in. After all, whatever had transpired or was in the process of transpiring between Greg and Lena complicated Betsy's feelings toward both men.

"Fancy meeting you here," Bill joked as he joined her at her table.

"We didn't *meet*." She eyed him. Bold move to sit without an invitation. Not a bad move. Just a bold one.

"Well, here we are. Sitting at the same table." He winked at her and situated himself. "We didn't get to talk much at Thanksgiving—which was a lovely affair. I really appreciate your taking me in, so to speak. Like a wet dog in the rain."

"A wet dog, huh?" She pursed her lips. "You're a dog, then, is that it? A hound dog?" Betsy dipped her chin and looked at him from beneath her lashes.

"A little bird told me you're hoping to make a local acquisition. Some property. Investment property, perhaps?"

Betsy frowned. "What's it to you? And, as a matter of fact, I've already *made* the acquisition. Signed the paperwork half an hour ago."

"I handle legal affairs for a number of businesses around town. The Pier, namely. Also, the gambling hall."

"You mean Nancy's place? You work for Nancy and Roy?"

He nodded, and Betsy's skin prickled into goose-flesh. Maybe her early instincts had been right. Maybe Bill was a good-looking slimeball after all. Maybe his protectiveness for his elderly neighbor... maybe none of that counted. Not if he was in cahoots with the town witch.

"Not exactly," he explained. "I'm an independent contractor. That's how the Pier treats me, too. I consult for a few hours a month. And as for the gambling hall, I'm hired by the county. Not the owners."

"So, you oversee them. Keep them in check?" Betsy asked, her ears perking up.

"Yes. More or less. They don't need me, though. That woman crosses her *I*s and dots her *T*s." He winked at Betsy. "Or whatever the expression is." Bill laughed and took a long sip of his coffee.

"I see," she said at length, taking in the information keenly. And that's how you came to learn about my ventures? Or rather, that's why you *care*?"

"I don't care—" he stopped short, pressing his palm to his chest "—well, in fact, I *do* care... about you—" He squeezed his eyes shut, smiled, and shook his head. "For-give me. That... that came out all wrong."

A waiter came by with a warm-up for Bill. "A second cup for you, ma'am?"

Betsy shook her head.

"What I meant," Bill went on, clearing his throat, "was that your business isn't my business. I just—I was trying to make conversation, I suppose."

"Oh, right. Right." She smiled to herself as she drank the last of her cup and pulled out her purse.

"Have you dabbled often in investment properties? Cemeteries?" he asked.

"No. I come from the business world, though. Travel agency. You might know of Book with Borden?"

"Oh sure, sure. That's you?" he leaned forward, and Betsy found herself mirroring his movement.

"Yes and no. My father opened it. A long time ago. I took over years back, and just recently I sold it. I wanted something... *different*. Something fresh."

"Cemeteries?"

She laughed at his point. "Well, with the cemetery, you see, there's a personal connection there. My friend is growing close with Norm. And the Garden Guild, as I mentioned before, is sort of... sponsoring the project as a charitable cause. We intend to plant flowers and bushes and help with the groundskeeping. We have big plans for it, in fact."

"Like what?" He stared at her earnestly, interestedly. Betsy felt his interest. In her bones and in her chest. In her heartbeat—her pulse.

"Right, um." She delayed, distracted momentarily by the fleeting memory of the last time she was on a date and how dramatically different it felt than this. "Well, we are going to add an access road—sort of the main gate, if you will, at the far end of Finch Street. Down past the Church's property by about an acre. As for parking, we intend to keep the lot modest. Something natural there, near where we'll erect the gate."

He nodded thoughtfully, and she went on.

"I had the idea of creating an actual garden—raised beds—in matching planters on either side of the gate. We could plant everything from thick bushes to flowers to herbs, even."

"An herb garden... at a *cemetery*?"

"Maybe even *in* the cemetery," Betsy corrected, smirking at him. "Haven't you heard? Take rosemary, for example. It symbolizes remembrance. What a nice addition. At least, that's one idea. Lots of life, you know? Texture. Colors. Smells. The whole of it. In planters and along the perimeter, naturally," she added.

"Wow." Bill leaned back and latched his hands behind his head. Betsy was forced to admire his torso, the girth of his biceps, the broad width of his shoulders as they stretched open, and she wondered what it might be like to be wrapped in those arms. In his height. "You know," he said, looking thoughtful, "when my mother died, I asked the funeral director if I could plant a rose bush on her grave. My mom, she loved roses."

"So do I," Betsy murmured in agreement.

"He said no." Bill released his hands and leaned in again. "That's *it*."

"What?" Betsy took a sip of her water, eyeing him over the top of the glass.

Bill's eyes glimmered. "That's just it, Betsy. I have an idea for your charitable venture. Your *gardening* project," he said, a broad smile flashing on his face. "You should get Norman's permission to plant things *on* the plots."

Betsy's heart skipped a beat. Excitement coursed through her veins, though whether it was attributable to Bill's idea or to his mere presence and attention... she couldn't be sure. "I think he *does* allow mourners to plant flowers. But they have to have them approved and so forth."

"Does his maintenance staff—groundskeepers, I mean—do they keep the flowers watered? Do they handle the pruning or whatever?" Bill leaned in even closer, his hands flat on the table. Big hands. Strong hands. Hands that didn't belong to a businessman. Hands that belonged to a *real* man.

Betsy replied, "I have no clue."

"That can be a huge draw. Not that you need to *market* a cemetery, mind you, but what if, when a family laid to rest a loved one, they had the option to plant something special there? Instead of fresh cut flowers..." he trailed off in time for Betsy to pick it up and run with it.

"Perennials. *Rosemary*."

"A rose bush," Bill replied, grinning.

"It's brilliant, Bill." She glanced at her watch. "Oh no. I'm *late*."

"Late?"

"My mom has a doctor's appointment. I was supposed to pick her up and drive her over. I'd better get going before she storms the club." Betsy rose and reached into her purse, but as she was about to pull out her wallet, Bill pointed past her.

"She's right there."

Betsy swiveled to see Lena raising her voice to someone in the lobby. She couldn't see the person.

"Uh oh," Betsy muttered, apologizing to Bill and starting off to talk the woman down. But as she made her way across the floor, she saw the back of the person on the receiving end of Lena's tirade.

"Greg." Bill was behind Betsy now. "It's just Greg."

"Well, that doesn't give her the right to ream him out," Betsy answered, indignant. "I don't know *what* her problem is with him, but enough is enough. I thought we were all on good terms."

"Betsy, wait."

She felt Bill's arm on her shoulder, tugging her back.

Frowning at him, she turned. "What?"

"It's—I just think we should let them sort it out. Give them a chance."

She narrowed her stare on Bill. "Do you *know* something?"

He held up his hands in defense. "It's none of my business."

Betsy hooked a finger toward him and lowered her voice, walking slowly back to their shared table so that he'd follow.

When they were down again, she settled her gaze and said, "Spill. *Now*."

"It's a lover's quarrel."

CHAPTER 27—EMILY

Mrs. Grimwood was worsening by the day. Emily began to fear the woman wouldn't make it to Christmas.

It was time to plan ahead, Emily decided. Norman gave a lot of attention to his mother, yes. But his time was stretched thin—between running Second Street and now preparing the Finch Street property (and for the town council meeting concerning just that), Emily knew that she'd need to take Christmas into her own hands.

In the time she'd lived in Gull's Landing, Emily had saved every penny, only spending money on groceries, rent, and her share of the utilities.

The moment had come to make good on a promise she'd made to herself when she first arrived in town. Therefore, on the afternoon of a perfectly chilly day, with Mrs. Grimwood tucked beneath a heavy quilt on the sofa, the television on but muted, and Norman running figures for the expansion project, Emily slipped outside and onto the sidewalk.

Her heavy coat kept her body warm, but the icy air cut her face like glass and by the time she made it to First Street, she couldn't feel her nose or her lips, and her cheeks stung from the dry, brittle cold.

The logical thing to do would be to start at *Cherise*, where she could warm up as she browsed.

Emily stood in front of the shop window for a beat too long, self-conscious, perhaps, about shopping in such a fine boutique. She blinked down at her outfit—a hand-me-down winter coat from her stepmother (something off of a clearance rack at Woolworth's). Beneath the coat, a ruddy long-sleeved blouse, jeans with threadbare knees, and socks that had long ago lost their elastic slumping into her sensible Keds. Sensible for their comfort, but not for the season. She'd have saved a nicer outfit for the day's trip to First Street, except they had a funeral planned for the coming weekend, and Emily knew better than to waste her good outfits early on in the week. Anyway, the heavy coat was practical and mature enough to hide her otherwise disappointing outfit.

She licked her lips then gripped the door handle, pausing half a moment before pulling it open and letting the warm shop suck her in.

Sliding between the window and a rack of tops, she opted to sort of hide as she shopped, praying the salesladies would ignore her like salesladies often did.

"Help you find anything today?" one called out just as Emily caressed a pretty silk scarf.

"Oh." Emily pressed a hand to her chest, startled. "Just browsing." She tried for as casual a smile as she could muster, but she knew it struck the wrong note when the woman lingered nearby.

Embarrassed, Emily held the scarf up for the woman's appraisal and said, hastily, "I'd like to buy this, please."

The woman gave her a brief once-over and then smiled. "Lovely choice. And would you care to continue *browsing*?" She dragged the last word out meaningfully, but Emily shook her head no and made her way to the cash register.

Once there, the saleswoman rang her order up. "That'll be thirty-four dollars and fifty-six cents," the woman sang out the numbers.

Emily's eyes bulged. Over thirty dollars for a scarf? But it was too late. She'd already committed. With a trembling hand, she reached into her pocket and withdrew the cash she'd taken out at the bank a day earlier, wistfully counting out a twenty-dollar bill, then a ten, then a five. Her gut clenched as she passed them over.

The woman slid the money from Emily's hand and counted it beside the register, making quick change then folding the scarf neatly into a thick sheet of tissue paper before dropping the bundle into an expensive shopping bag and dangling the whole, feather-light purchase above the countertop. "Thanks for shopping at *Cherise*," she chirped. "Come back *real* soon, sweetie."

Emily thanked her and all but sprinted out, mortified over the whole process.

After that, according to her carefully calculated budget, Emily had less than twenty dollars left of her Christmas budget. A total of fifteen dollars and fifty-four cents for all the gifts she had in mind to buy her new friends. For the ingredients to Christmas recipes she wanted to try out. For something special for Mrs. Grimwood. Something *meaningful*.

Deciding for good to pass up the opportunity to indulge in a fancy meal at Maeve's, Emily walked up to Geppetto's, its window display now decked in thick garland and colorful Christmas lights. Cottony faux snow lay beneath the feet of the dolls and toy trucks on the wooden shelf just beyond the glass.

Emily let out a sigh. She didn't need a doll, even if she wanted one. Still, she walked into the store.

A voice caught her off guard just as she stepped onto the burgundy carpet. "I know you!"

"Mrs.... Shytle?" Emily screwed her face up, pretending it took her a moment to place the woman.

"And you know me, it would seem!" she cried in reply, drifting from her spot in front of a shelf of porcelain-faced Madame Alexander dolls.

Emily tore her gaze away from the pretty things, but try as she might, she wasn't able to muster a smile for the acerbic woman.

"From the Garden Guild," Emily prompted, preserving her secret—the one about how she was sworn to hate Nancy for trying to build a second cemetery.

"Or the mortuary," Nancy pointed out. "You work for Norman, right? At Second Street?" Nancy's addition of *Second Street* came out pinched, as though it was meant to be a reminder that Mr. Grimwood's place of business was just that: a singular *place* on a singular *road* in Gull's Landing. A reminder that there might be more than just the one cemetery... one day.

Indeed, if that *was* the woman's implication, well, she was right. Mum was the word, however.

"The Garden Guild, however," Nancy went on. "When's our next meeting?"

Emily forced down her compulsion to repeat the word *our* and instead shrugged and furrowed her brow, feigning an attempt to conjure the details. She blinked away her false confusion and offered, "January? I think?" In truth, the new and improved Garden Guild met all the time. A few times a week. For Bingo night or margaritas or a chilly beach walk or a night at the movies. Come spring, those get-togethers would double, no doubt. Once the weather warmed and it was time to really work on their gardening projects, of course.

"January. Hm." The woman tapped an ovaline, French-tipped nail on her chin. "That's the thing about this little *club*, you know—oh, honey, what was your name?"

"Emily."

"*Emily*, of course. What a pretty name. As I was saying —it's so difficult to keep a club going when it's *seasonal*. You see what I mean, surely. What's there to do for a gardening club in the winter? Particularly in Jersey, of all places?" She shook her head and clicked her tongue.

Apparently, Emily thought to herself, this woman knew *nothing* about gardening. Anyone with a brain in her head knew that gardening was about the cold season. The sowing season. The hard work—clearing last season's weeds and planting the seeds—it was critical. Nancy's confession made all the sense in the world, and, for some reason, this put Emily at ease. Like a landmark along the grid of streets in Gull's Landing, Emily could slot Nancy Shytle neatly into her position in society. Just as Emily had a place there. And Betsy Borden. And even an oddball like Lil.

Emily's gaze lifted past Nancy to the row of dolls, her heart aching to touch one. To fluff the dress and rub her thumb on the painted cheek.

Nancy followed her stare. "Do you collect, sweetheart?"

"Collect?" Emily frowned.

"Madame Alexander dolls? My daughter collects them. She's fifteen, but age has no bearing on a young lady's interests, as it shouldn't. Nothing should have any bearing on a woman's interests, in fact." Emily still wasn't sure what the woman meant, and her face must have communicated as much, because Nancy explained herself. "Here's a little secret for you, *Emily*." The woman dropped her voice low and dipped her chin conspiratorially. "In this world, a woman must fight for what she wants. And she shouldn't let *anything* get in her way."

CHAPTER 28—LIL

The December town council meeting started in exactly five minutes, and Norman was hyperventilating in the men's room of the town hall.

Lil coaxed him through the door. "It's going to be *fine*, Norm. We just need to barrel through."

And it would have been fine, too, if Nancy Shytle hadn't shown up. But naturally, she had. She and her useless husband, Roy.

That's what sent Norman into panic mode.

Lil regretted telling him all about her history with Nancy Shytle. She regretted it sorely, especially now.

"Norm, we've got to go in. They'll be starting. Listen, all you have to do is read from the notes we wrote up. That's it. The rest is in the hands of Mayor Brooks and the council members. Easy."

The door fell away from Lil's face and Norman appeared. His color had returned, and his breath was steadier now. He let out a sigh. "Okay. If you say so, Lil."

A softness returned to his eyes, and Lil would have kissed him. She would have. In another life. Another world. Another place. But for now, the eyes of the town were watching, through wooden doors and all—they were watching. And Lil knew she had no room to make a mistake.

"Norman Grimwood of Second Street Mortuary," the mayor announced.

Norman rose and made his way up the narrow passage to the podium, where Betsy and Nancy had stood a month before.

"Mayor Brooks, council members," Norman began. And then, before their very eyes, he gave an even-keeled, firm overview of the acquisition of the land behind the church, the agreement with St. Gertrude's, the onboarding of Betsy as a financial backer, and the report of the early progress on the old Finch Street potter's field.

When he'd finished, he gave a curt, confident nod, adjusted his glasses and waited.

Lil was proud of him. And of herself and her little group of girlfriends. Together, they all made quite the team.

Mayor Brooks cleared his throat. "Well, then," he began, leaning his weight into the wooden cabinet and speaking directly into the microphone. "It would appear that there is no need for a second burial business in town. Mrs. Shittle, the town surely appreciates your willingness to take the project on, but at this time, I'll have to decline your proposal."

If there'd been a gavel within reach, Lil suspected the portly man might have banged it on the wood. That was the feeling in the room after Norman's presentation and Mayor Brooks' quick move to approve it. Anticipation and then *victory*.

But it wasn't his so-called verdict that came as the biggest shock that night.

Oh, no.

The biggest shock was when, after the rest of the town proceedings, Nancy Shytle rose from her seat in the front row, held out a porcelain hand to Norman, shook it, then smiled at Mayor Brooks and said, "In that case, I'm off to my next project. Too-da-loo, everyone!"

In like a lion.

And out like a lamb.

At least, that was how it appeared.

Just a couple of weeks later, and Lil's life had taken on a new normal.

Now, instead of waking up and wondering what might happen to her on any given day, she awoke with a purpose. Every day. Lil Gulch had a *purpose*.

With sporadic snowfall, it wasn't yet possible to clear the new lot; however, Lil, Betsy, and Emily had started working to collect seed packets, compile gardening tools, and research plants worthy of hallowed ground.

Additionally, Lena agreed to organize a catalogue for prospective clients—information and photographs of the plants and flowers they might choose for their loved ones' plots.

Norman hired Bill to help coordinate a legal effort to

ensure that proper licenses, permits, and other formalities were in place for a spring opening. Of course, they didn't intend to have a party or a celebration once the new cemetery was in working order; however, the group had decided together to begin offering plots as early as May. This would allow for a smoother transition away from Second Street.

The only issue remaining, as related to the business affairs, was what to name the new cemetery.

Norman had already turned Betsy down on her Borden Boneyard idea, reminding her that funeral matters were serious. Betsy had said she was as serious as a heart attack and that when she died, she fully expected them to engrave "Here lie the bones of Betsy Borden" across her granite headstone.

"Embed some diamonds in there, while you're at it," she declared over eggnog on Christmas Day. "And I think I'd like an evergreen. Can we do evergreens on the plots?" Betsy lifted a bough of the Christmas tree standing in the corner of the Grimwood living room, where they had all congregated to exchange presents and enjoy a hearty dinner.

"I'm not sure about that one," Emily replied, her face earnest. Since the town council had given their approval, Emily was in overdrive trying to get things organized. She'd gripped life with a new energy, it seemed like to Lil. A ferocious focus. Every idea they had, she jotted down and followed through on. Every question, Emily would find an answer.

"Well, I need *something* to look forward to in the afterlife," Betsy joked. But it fell flat. Ever since the beginning of the month, something had changed in Betsy. And Lena, too.

Bill and Greg had been out of the picture, not that they were ever fastly *in* the picture. But gone were Betsy's gripes about the nerd in his sexy red car, terrorizing the neighborhood with his arrogance and allure. Gone, too, were Lena's playful spats with the kindly, white-haired man with elbow patches on his sweaters who whistled through his teeth like a little old grandfather.

The two men had all but disappeared from Bingo nights, and when Lil had invited both to Christmas at the Grimwoods', they'd kindly declined, citing prior engagements.

"Speaking of the afterlife," Norman interjected, "we have some news for Emily."

Lil shifted her gaze to Norman across the table. He was swirling his glass of wine, his expression pensive. She flicked a glance to Irma, who was in no better but no worse shape of late. Medications and proper attention had held her up well. Lil sensed that the holidays and Emily's affection had helped, adding to what must have been a monotonous, tiresome life.

Trying for Norman's attention, Lil discreetly slid her foot across the floor and tapped his shoe. He glanced up at her, lowering his glass as his cheeks turned pink. She smiled. It was meant to be a motherly smile, and she expected Norman to return a fatherly one. Not that Lil and Norman were officially *together*. And of course, Emily was not their child. But that's how the relationship had progressed between the three. Paternal and maternal over Emily. Protective. Proud. Sometimes amused, like now.

"Don't tell us you're dying, too," Lena snorted.

"Ma!" Betsy cried. "What'sa matter with you!"

Lil and Norman exchanged a shake of their heads, and Lil couldn't help but steal a quick look at Irma, who'd evidently missed what Lena had said or was enjoying the broccoli soup enough to disregard Lena. Then again, perhaps even Irma had grown used to Lena's continual brashness.

Norman cleared his throat. "It has to do with the future of Second Street."

Lil beamed at their shared secret and looked at Emily to see if she might guess.

But before either Emily or Norman could say more, the doorbell chimed.

"Were we expecting anyone else?" Betsy asked, suspicious.

Norman rose from his seat on the sofa. "Could be Bill. I reminded him he was welcome to come by."

"He and Greg are eating at the Club," Lena offered flatly. "No way they'll show up. Not after—"

"Ma, hush," Betsy shot. Lil glared meaningfully at Betsy, who ignored her.

But when Lil looked at Emily, hoping to recruit her help in dragging the truth out of Betsy, she saw the girl's face had turned ashen.

"Emily? Are you okay? You look like you're going to faint," Lil pointed out.

Voices drifted from the front door.

Emily pushed up from the floor, where she sat with an unopened gift in her lap, and shifted the pretty box back beneath the tree, smoothing her black dress and furrowing her brow. "I'll be right back," she murmured.

CHAPTER 29—EMILY

As she neared the door, her worst fear came true.

"Jimmy," Emily whispered.

Norman lifted his hand. "Emily, stay there," he commanded, his tone sharp and his voice deep. Emily had never heard Norman speak that way. Even when he was harsh about something to do with the funeral home, or impatient with someone's error... he sounded *different*. Strong. In control.

She stared at her husband, trying to swallow past the hard lump in her throat.

"I have a right to talk to my *wife*," Jimmy shot back. Emily studied him. He looked no different than when she'd left him months earlier. Ratty jeans and a smokey leather jacket she could smell from yards off. His hair greasy and falling into his eyes as he pointed a dirty fingernail at Emily. "It's Christmas, and we want her back. Back in Wildwood."

Emily folded her arms over her chest and hugged herself.

"Whatever you have to say to her, you can say from right there on my stoop. What's more, I'll give you two minutes to say it and then you will leave, young man," Norman directed. His words, coupled with his deepened, threatening voice, left no room for an argument.

Emily found a reply. "I'm not coming home, Jimmy. And I want you to sign the divorce papers. I want you to do that right away. It's over."

Behind her, Betsy, Lil, and Lena huddled around Emily, bolstering her confidence and giving her the extra oomph she needed to keep from collapsing at the sight of Jimmy.

"I'm not signing the papers, and I don't gotta," Jimmy shot back, sneering then snickering as he took a step backwards and toward the stoop. He pointed his finger again at Emily. "And your old man's on my side. If we get a divorce, you can kiss him and your stepmom goodbye. And anything they owe you. He told me as much. If you divorce me, you lose it *all*, Emily."

But it was Emily's turn to snicker and sneer. "You say that as if I *have* something to lose."

Jimmy took a step down onto the second step. "It sure looks like you have something to lose," Jimmy lifted both hands and with each index finger drew a square around the Grimwood home.

Norman turned to the girls. "Lil, call the police," he instructed.

Lil squeezed Emily's shoulder then walked to the phone.

But Jimmy was holding up his hands. "I'm leaving. It's not the police you'll need to win this, Emily *Addams*." He sucked in a snort and hocked up spit into the snow-blanketed hedges. "By law, I don't have to sign jack *squat*."

"He's right," Betsy cut in. "We don't need the police, Norman. We need a lawyer."

CHAPTER 30—BETSY

The last person Betsy wanted to talk to on Christmas Day was Bill. Especially after what he'd done to her.

Still, Emily needed something greater than a funeral director, or a widow, or a businesswoman such as Betsy, or anyone else in the gang could offer. Emily needed a way to get free of that horrid husband.

"Norman, will you call Bill?" Betsy asked in hushed tones when Lil and Lena swept Emily back into the living room.

"Of course. I'll call him now. See what he can do or suggest."

Betsy nodded and thanked him, pouring fresh mugs of eggnog and carrying them in to the ladies who sat cooing over the poor, stricken girl.

"Emily, what did you *see* in him?" Betsy asked, once Emily was tucked onto the sofa next to Irma, who caressed her arm in a grandmotherly, loving way.

"A way out," Emily mumbled back, drawing another

sip of her drink. "The same thing I've looked for since I was a little girl."

"A way out," Lil affirmed, sighing meaningfully. "I can understand that."

"We all can," Lena added.

Betsy narrowed her gaze on her mother. "Was John a *way out*? Or was that Greg?"

All eyes turned to Betsy.

Lena, whose feathers had never ruffled once in her life simply shrugged. "Each was for a different reason."

Emily asked, "What do you mean?"

Betsy set her jaw and crossed her arms, leaning back into the sitting chair in the corner of the room. It wasn't her place to divulge her mother's secret. It wasn't her place to explain that Bill had spilled the beans to her in a matter of moments—a lifetime of secrets uttered matter-of-factly on a charging walk over to Lena and Greg in the lobby of the club. If Bill's inability to read people was *that* pronounced, Betsy couldn't see how they could carry on in some degree of flirtation, no matter how preliminary.

Lena answered Emily as simply as she'd agreed with Lil previously, but there was a hitch in her expression, the suggestion, at least, that Lena understood the gravity of her words. That she understood the implication for Betsy. That everything Betsy knew to be true... was *false*. That her past wasn't her past. It was a mystery.

"Well, the cat's been out of the bag for weeks, now. So, I suppose it's only fair to tell you all. Greg Rosen was—*is*, I suppose—Betsy's natural father."

Emily and Lil gasped in synchrony. Even Irma's mouth fell ajar, and Irma had been somewhat separated from the drama of their friend group. Protected in the shroud of her illness from the woes of others. Relative to cancer, Betsy's paternity was no big deal, probably.

For her part, Betsy sat limply, still unmoored by the news, even after weeks of trying to come to grips with it.

Once several shocked moments passed, Lena cleared the silence. "I was young and taken with the man of my dreams," she murmured blissfully.

"John Borden?" Irma managed, coughing mildly and clearing her throat at length.

Lena's smile fell off and she shook her head. "This smart fellow who was earning his teaching credentials at the time. Greg Rosen. But he had two strikes against him in my mother's eyes." Lena smirked.

"One, he didn't go to our church. But that was less problematic to her. The real issue was Greg's chosen career field."

"Teaching," Betsy added with a twinge of repugnance.

"It wasn't what my parents saw for me. And by the time I'd fallen in love with Greg, John's parents and mine were already planning our wedding."

"Why didn't you speak up?" Emily asked.

"Even if it was with John, marriage could be a way out. I thought maybe I could squirrel away some money and take a bus up to Greg. It was all very romantic in my mind," Lena ruminated, her red fingernails flashing as she twirled her wrist, rewinding the tape to the memories of her earlier life. "I'd sacrifice myself at the altar, so to speak. Marry John. Formulate a plan and escape. To be with Greg."

"And Greg? He... he helped you with your plan?"

Lena shook her head. "He didn't lift a finger. He left and began his career, and I never heard from him again. Until he moved back to Gull's Landing last year."

"And Betsy?" Lil asked.

"The timing worked out well enough," Lena admitted. "When Betsy came along, the doctors deemed her premature. Premature enough to be John's. There was no question. Ever."

"My brunette hair—" Betsy twirled a lock around her finger. "Always did wonder about that."

"It could have come from anywhere." Her mother waved her off.

"Why did you never say anything, Ma?"

"What difference would it have made, buttercup?" Lena shrugged.

"He's nice," Emily offered thoughtfully. "I like Greg. I like Bill, too."

"Bill's worse than Greg." Betsy blew air through her lips. "At least Greg didn't shatter my world with an out-of-the-blue revelation about my real dad."

"Shatter your world? If learning that shattered your world, then it was pretty fragile." Irma coughed into her handkerchief and Betsy paled, swallowing hard.

"You're right," she replied. "It's just—it's a big thing. To learn it at this age? That some stranger is my dad? That my mother never loved my father?"

"I loved John. I loved him so much I never told Greg about Betsy," Lena shared with the others.

Betsy shivered at hearing this all over again.

"Does he know now?" Emily asked, rapt.

Betsy nodded, but Lena answered. "When John died,

I sent him a letter. Out of grief, mostly. I just said he had a daughter."

"Wait," Lil interjected. "How can you be sure Betsy was Greg's?"

Lena dipped her chin toward Lil. "I *knew*. Believe me. A woman *knows*."

Betsy sighed. "He started his trek back here then, making a plan to work through his tenure until retirement then buy a place near Lena. He made good on it, moving right into our very own *neighborhood*."

"It's like you had two fathers," Emily pointed out. "Two nice ones, too."

"You got your business sense from John," Lena added. "And your sweetness from Greg. That's what I've always figured."

"And your stubbornness from Lena, no doubt," Lil joked, laughing. Betsy smiled, her stomach unclenching for the first time in weeks. Maybe her friends were right.

Maybe it wasn't the end of the world.

She could forgive her mother—of course she could. She could forgive Greg. Particularly since he hadn't even known about Betsy until recently.

But Bill—

"And what does Bill have to do with all of this?" Lil asked, lifting the thought out of Betsy's mind and spinning it into being.

"Greg hired him to handle his estate, and they got to talking and Bill moved in here, sort of warming to Greg as though Greg was a father figure to Bill, too," Betsy replied, her tone softening.

Even so, she felt cool toward him. Too cool. Too cold. Too hurt.

"Let's open presents," Betsy declared, changing the subject. "Then we can talk about what we're going to do with this ratty old Jimmy guy."

CHAPTER 31—LIL

Norman returned from the kitchen and the phone call to his lawyer-friend, presumably.

"Speaking of Bill," Lil addressed Norman, "what did he say on the phone?"

"He's happy to help Emily secure a divorce and even a restraining order, should she need it."

Lil couldn't help but gasp faintly. "A restraining order?" She glanced at Emily. "Do you think you need that?"

Betsy replied for Emily. "He tracked Emily down *here*. Of course she needs it. Bill's right."

Lil caught a flicker in Betsy's expression. A crack in the facade of her determination to loathe the lawyer. But she ignored it in order to focus on the task at hand. "Good point. How *did* he find you?"

Emily shrugged in reply. "I mean, I sort of ran away, sure. But it was no secret. I told my stepmother I found employment with the funeral director in Gull's Landing."

"Oh." Lil and Betsy exchanged a sorrowful look. It

was easy to forget how young Emily was. How, despite her maturity and despite her work ethic, when it came down to it, she was just a girl. Trying to make her way in life and do things right. Right for herself and right for others.

"What else did Bill say?" Betsy asked Norman. "I mean, how can he represent Emily if he does gambling law? They're two separate things."

Norman answered easily. "Oh, no. Bill does it all. He covers finance law, gambling law, family law, estate planning—the man is like a variety show of legal know-how. Has all these different licenses or whatever. It's no wonder the guy is busy today. He must've been invited to a million holiday parties," Norman replied. "Even so, I invited him to drop by. He accepted this time."

Lil's gaze flew to Betsy, who pursed her lips.

"We've finished dinner," Betsy pointed out.

Norman shrugged, aloof to the nuances of a woman's protests, as men usually were. "He'll have a drink and be on his way, but he says he can talk to Emily today and get the ball rolling quickly if she'd like."

Norman's intentions were innocent and entirely concerned with Emily.

But Lil wondered if Bill had an ulterior motive for accepting a *second* invitation to be near Betsy.

She also wondered if Betsy wouldn't put her foot down. After all, in a matter of weeks, Bill had become nothing less than an enemy to her. An antagonist.

So, it surprised Lil when Betsy responded on Emily's behalf. "Sounds like a matter we ought to handle now, before that rat-tailed jerk returns to Gull's Landing. Don't you think, Emily?"

Emily, who was more attuned to the little intricacies of their recent conversation, lowered her voice. "Only if you're comfortable seeing him, Betsy."

Betsy nodded and crossed the room to her mother on the hearth, lowering and grabbing the woman's hand. "I think we can handle it. There are worse things in life than having two men love you."

Her double-speak wasn't lost on Lil. And it wasn't meant as a put-down for the others—for Lil, whom they didn't even realize was loved by Norman. Nor was it a putdown for Emily, who herself had enjoyed the affections of two men, not to mention those of her father. Perhaps there was something to Betsy's quick acceptance.

Lil looked at Betsy and asked, "You forgive him then? For spilling the beans?"

But it was Lena who answered. "*Forgive* Bill? He did nothing wrong. If you've got someone to be mad at, at least pick me. I'm the one who never told you the truth, Betsy."

Betsy's chest rose with a deep breath. "We have a choice in this world," she began.

Norman settled into his seat next to Lil. Irma and Emily shifted into a better position on the couch. The fire crackled behind Betsy and Lena, who sat off to the side of it, their backs toasty, no doubt.

When Betsy didn't immediately explain herself, Lil prompted her. "G'head," she said. "We have a choice in this world?"

As she answered, Betsy's focus narrowed on Lil, or at

least, that's how it felt. "You can choose to be mad at someone—you can *choose* to be angry. Or... you can choose the other path. The path of forgiveness."

The others sort of oohed and awed at the clever insight. Nearly biblical, Betsy had nailed it on the head.

But she went on, smirking and swirling her eggnog with her bejeweled hand. "I just can't be angry with Bill. He's too damn sexy."

As THEY WAITED for Bill to arrive, they took turns opening gifts from one another.

Norman gave Lil a poinsettia plant with an ornament tucked into the foil-wrapped pot. The glass globe was laced over in purple lilies. "Oh Norman," Lil breathed. "It's perfect."

She passed him a wrapped stack of crossword puzzles and a ballpoint pen engraved with his initials, which he said he'd cherish. As for the crosswords, well, she could only hope he'd share them.

For Irma, Lil had crocheted a warm winter cap, something to help fight off the chill as winter grew bleaker, turning the corner into the new year. Lil wasn't much with a crochet hook, but Irma seemed to love the thoughtful gift.

Lil then gave Betsy and Lena a set of sherry glasses and a bottle of the stuff, laughing along as Lena joked that she didn't need another reason to imbibe.

For Emily, Lil had baked a batch of cheesecake chocolate chip cookies, complete with a cookie jar she'd purchased in an antiques store on First Street.

"These look like the ones in the bakery on First Street," Emily marveled, tipping the dish this way and that.

"They must have stolen my recipe, then," Lil warned. "No one I know makes cheesecake cookies. I'll have to have a word with the owner." She smiled good naturedly, but something shone in Emily's eyes. Gratitude, perhaps. Gratitude from the depths of her little heart.

Betsy passed out her gifts next.

For Norman, an ornament in the shape of a casket. Inside, a gift card to the local nursery. "To get us started at the second graveyard," she said.

"A coffin ornament?" He dangled it in the air. "A little macabre, wouldn't you say?"

Lil replied for Betsy. "You're a funeral director, Norm. What's more macabre than that?"

He chuckled and thanked Betsy, who passed a wrapped package to Irma. "This one, Irma, is from all of us. Lena, Lil, Emily and me."

The old woman carefully peeled away the wrapping paper, revealing gobs of tissue paper until the woman pulled out a white envelope. She opened the envelope, her bony hands trembling. "What's this?" Irma asked, lifting a white card from the envelope.

"It's a service, you see. The girls and I hired you an attendant. Someone to be here with you while Emily and Norman are at work. She'll cook and clean and tend to you. Whatever you need. Five days a week. It's more than just the palliative nursing you receive. It's everything you could need."

Irma's eyes welled up and her lower jaw rolled as her mouth worked the right thing to say. But Betsy stood and crossed to her, taking the old woman's face in her hands. "Don't say a thing. You need this, and you'll have it. It'll give you a break and company and anyway, I'll swing by sometimes to check in on you. Lena, too. Right, Ma?"

Lena waved her hand. "Of course, of course."

"So will I," Lil chimed in.

Irma would begin treatments on January second. Norman had shared the word from her doctors—that she'd need around-the-clock care if it was to go well. That's when they all got together to decide that they'd make it happen for her. For Irma. For Norman. For all of them.

"It's as much a gift for us as it is for you, Irma," Lil went on.

Norman was pushing tears from his cheeks, his glasses foggy and his body hunched. Lil wrapped an arm around his shoulders. "When a person is sick, the people who love that person get sick, too." She knew this from experience, though her experience wasn't a perfect match —her love for Sam had been diluted to the point of nonexistence. "We get worried. Troubled. Heartsick." Lil wiped tears from her eyes now, too.

Betsy sniffled. "Okay, enough of all this. It's supposed to be a happy day."

"Sometimes you get a little sad even on happy days," Emily pointed out through tears.

"Before any of us die, how's about we keep opening

presents?" Lena croaked from the rocking chair she'd moved to.

"Oh, *Ma*, you know how to kill the moment," Betsy groaned.

Irma, however, laughed. A belly laugh, full and happy and so hard that she should have launched into a coughing fit. But by the grace of God, for that moment, she didn't cough. Not once. As though her new treatment had already been administered and its effects glorious, she only laughed.

CHAPTER 32—EMILY

"This one is to Lil from Betsy." Emily passed the brown paper package tied up with strings to Lil, who cautiously untied the string and lifted the corners of the wrapping to reveal a box.

"*Cherise*?" Lil asked, her thumb caressing the label on the corner of the white cardboard.

"It's the only place to get something nice," Betsy replied. "Let me know if it doesn't fit. I saved the receipt."

Lil lifted a white bathing suit from the tissue paper and marveled at it. "You *know* me," she said breathlessly. "My favorite season, my favorite outfit."

"There's more," Betsy pointed out.

Lil pulled out a white, lacy swim cover. "Oh, Betsy. You shouldn't have."

"I didn't take much of a risk. I just figure you're the sort who likes what she likes, ya know?"

Lil smiled and nodded. "Now I can have two of each. Nearly matching. And—yes. I do *like* what I like, I suppose."

"Your turn, Em," Betsy handed her a box, too, and Emily steeled herself for what may be inside. No one knew Emily. Even her own family didn't know her deepest desires. The promises she made to herself. The ones she broke. The things she wanted in life. Betsy would have no way of knowing that she, too, would love to own something fancy from *Cherise*.

When she removed the brown paper to see another *Cherise* box, her heart bounced low in her stomach. She glanced hopefully at Betsy who raised her eyebrows.

"Now, Emily, I can't pin down your sense of fashion quite yet, so I hope you won't mind—"

But before Betsy could finish, Emily saw that there was no garment folded carefully within the tissue. No accessory.

Just a white envelope. She frowned and plucked it from its nest among the thick white paper. Emily swallowed as she opened the flap and tugged out a long rectangular piece of cardstock. Her eyes flew across the words then up to Betsy. "Oh, Betsy. This is too much."

Betsy waved her off. "No, it's not. You go and pick something out. A few somethings, actually. Then wear them for us to see so I can get a sense of your style. Then next year, when Christmas comes around again, I can buy you a duplicate of something you already own, too!"

The others laughed, but not Emily. A knot formed in her throat, keeping her from murmuring so much as a thank-you.

But as the others laughed and moved on to the next round of gifts, Emily and Betsy locked eyes. The latter returned a small smile and dip of her chin, and Emily knew that Betsy knew that she was very, very grateful.

"Okay, it's my turn now." Emily shook her head and forced herself to focus. "I, um, well—it was hard to shop for you all this year," she confessed. "I had a bit of a flub while I was out and about and—" she swallowed "—anyway," she shoved small gift bags at each person, humiliated, really. "It's not much. I'm terribly sorry."

Betsy withdrew hers first, a small ceramic pot with a single sprout, just two weeks old and barely hovering above the soil line. "A rosebush. You said your favorite flower—"

Betsy cut Emily off. "Roses. Oh Emily, this is the most *thoughtful* gift in the world. Thank you."

Lena withdrew hers, too. A larger pot. No sprout.

"It's a bulb, Emily said softly. "A daffodil."

"My *favorite*," Lena answered, admiring the earthen chamber. "And where did you find this?"

"The nursery," Emily replied as evenly as she could muster. She didn't confess it was from their clearance greenhouse. A little plastic tent out back of the indoor growing room. The others didn't notice her omission, however, and just cooed.

"Mr. Grimwood," Emily went on as Norman lifted a container from his bag. "That one is for you and Irma," she pointed out. "Rosemary," she added.

"For remembrances," Norman murmured.

Lil was pulling her pot from her bag now. "What's this?" she asked Emily gently. "A lily?"

"You said you prefer useful plants. Something to eat

or something hardy," Emily pointed out bashfully. "It's a palomino grape vine. Or, at least it *will* be. Next spring."

"A palomino grape vine?" Lil marveled. "Where in the world did you find *this*? And—"

"Just inland of Ocean City," Emily replied. "I took the bus. There's a vineyard there, and they sell saplings. It's sort of a—well, just meant to be a souvenir. But I figure you can start your own little grapevine on your fence or wherever you'd like. Sherry is made from palomino grapes," Emily added proudly.

"It'll go in the cemetery," Lil announced. "It'll go right next to the sign. Or on it even. Oh, Emily. It's *perfect*. Thank you."

Emily beamed, but she had one more gift to pass out. It'd be awkward, now that everyone seemed settled and each of the gifts was fair. She'd tucked the remaining gift bag in the far back of the tree, so as to keep it a bit of a secret. A finale, even. But with Irma studying the rosemary sapling and Norman standing and stretching, the moment was gone. Passed. And it was too late.

"We have one more thing—" Norman announced. "A gift for Emily from the rest of us."

She frowned. "For *me*?" Emily's cheeks blazed red. She'd hate to get a group gift. And what could it be anyway?

"Here." Norman thrust a folder at Emily.

She frowned, examining it with confusion. "Gull's Landing Community College?" she looked up.

"Open it," Lil prodded.

Emily did, and inside she found brochures for general admission, student life, and the Mortuary Sciences

Program. And an application Emily shook her head. "What—I—?"

"Krueger is retiring next spring. We need a replacement, and Emily—I'd love for that to be you. Technically, I can run embalming while you intern under me. But only if you want to. No pressure, we're all chipping in to cover tuition." His voice was firm and unyielding, but Emily nodded slowly.

Never in her life had she imagined attending college. It just wasn't in the cards for her. Something far out of her reach—in a different orbit, even. Beyond the veil of possibility for Wildwood-born, twice-married, once-divorced Emily.

But this... this could be *everything*. Not only would Emily have a job... she was about to have a *career*. In the place she'd made home.

She first hugged Irma, gripping the woman gently but passionately, kissing her on the cheek before she tore away and hugged Mr. Grimwood, too, gushing thanks.

"Norman, please. I think it's time you called me Norman."

"Norman," Emily echoed. "Everyone—" she lifted her voice across the room. "You can't know what this means to me. Thank you all."

The others smiled and hugged Emily just as the doorbell rang—again.

CHAPTER 33—BETSY

"Paperboy!" A voice rang out from the front hall.

"Paperboy?" Betsy smirked. "Gee," she went on sarcastically, "I wonder who *that* could be?"

Norman called out for Bill to join them and he walked into the living room.

Indeed, Bill was holding that morning's edition of the Gull's Landing Gazette. He slapped it on his palm. "Merry Christmas, everyone! Somebody forgot to check the stoop," he shook the thickly rolled packet of black and white print.

"Funny, I went out to get it this morning but got distracted. Lil showed up," Norman laughed nervously.

"It was actually wedged in the crook of your hedges. You might want to file a formal complaint with whoever oversees that kid's route. It was a terrible aim," Bill joked.

"Where's Greg?" Lena asked as the rocking chair creaked beneath her.

Betsy wanted to shoot her a look, but she thought better of it.

"At home, I'd imagine. Believe it or not, he and I are *not* conjoined at the hip," Bill joked.

Betsy raised her eyebrows. "Did he at least... did he have somewhere to go today?"

"We had dinner at the club last night, and he told me this morning he'd take it easy." Bill unsnapped the rubber band from the paper and let it flap open on the coffee table. "I think he doesn't much mind the solitude. If anything, it's me who needs company."

Betsy nodded and saw her mother purse her lips. She made a mental note to drop her mother by Greg's house later on. Couldn't hurt.

"Emily," Bill said, "are you okay?"

Taking it upon herself to answer for her friend, Betsy stood. "She needs to get a divorce from this guy. And she needs a protective order, too. Isn't that right, Emily?" Betsy opened a hand to the girl.

Emily nodded meekly. "I had him served with a divorce months ago, but he refuses to sign. I just went through the county to do it. I had to pay a fee and everything." Her words dripped in pain, and Betsy felt for the girl. This was exactly why Betsy had never married. Divorce could be brutal. She'd seen it too many times with her friends.

There were other reasons, too. Betsy just hadn't known what they were, really. With the revelation about her confused parentage, she thought she'd figured them out. It was like the truth had always lived in Betsy's heart, niggling at her. The truth that her mother had married the wrong man... or that she'd married the right one, but it was already too late. How Lena had lived with herself all those years... it was a wonder to Betsy that she kept her spirits up. But perhaps there was more to the woman's cutting exterior than strength. Sometimes, humor and sarcasm and raw honesty—sometimes a woman had to use those things to shield her heart when it was more fragile than anyone could understand.

At least, that's what Betsy had come to know in the preceding weeks. That's why it wasn't her mother she took fault with, but Bill, for tearing away the shield and leaving Lena—and therefore Betsy—exposed to the truth. Naked when they didn't need to be. Bare.

"I'll handle everything. It'll be no problem." Bill popped a handful of caramel popcorn from the coffee table into his mouth and lowered comfortably onto the sofa. He wore a forest green sweater vest over a white button-down. His jeans were snug but flattering, and his loafers reminded her of something John Borden had worn on his days off.

Even though it might be Bill's day off, here he was, ready to work.

Maybe he and Betsy had more in common than she realized.

"Why don't you two take the kitchen," Norman suggested. "You can work out your plan, and we'll finish up in here."

Emily looked at Betsy, who read her mind. "I'll come with you," Betsy said. "It always helps to have a friend in hard stuff like this."

Emily went ahead, carrying her mug of eggnog, but as Betsy started to follow, Bill grabbed her elbow and together they ducked into the hallway.

"What?" Betsy hissed, glancing beyond him to see Emily disappear into the kitchen.

"Listen, I'm sorry, Betsy," Bill replied, his voice barely audible. "I didn't know you *didn't know*. When I met Greg, he told me he had one goal and one goal alone, to piece back the life he left behind. To me, it sounded as though you and Lena were in the loop, just hard eggs to crack."

Betsy scoffed. "I don't know what that's supposed to mean... I've been kind to him since the day I met him—at the club."

"But you decided against extending me that same kindness? From the get-go, you've been cool to me, Betsy."

She swallowed. "We can't talk about this now. Emily's waiting."

"Let me make it up to you, Betsy. Okay? One date. Maeve's or that Italian place on the boardwalk. I owe you that much for changing your world."

Betsy had no choice, really she didn't. Either she argued with him and delayed their meeting with Emily even longer. Or she agreed.

"It's a date."

CHAPTER 34—LIL

Pleased with both ends of the gift exchange and the fact that they had a game plan for Emily—and the future at large—Lil inched closer to Norman on the loveseat, her pinky finger brushing against his.

Irma and Lena chatted about any number of things—perhaps Lena was explaining the recent drama with Greg, for one. The fire crackled nearby, and life was perfect. Lil had all that she wanted. Even if she and Norman didn't move beyond an intimate courtship into something more formal, she was content.

And he was, too.

They murmured about plans for the cemetery, easily hopping from topic to topic, their arrangement comfortable, sitting close enough that their thighs touched. The thrill of their proximity and the hope for the future gave Lil great peace. And she suspected it gave Norman peace, too, based on the fact that he called her every night and sent her flowers every Saturday.

"New Year's Eve," Norman said, changing the subject more dramatically.

"Yes?" Lil asked.

"What are our plans?" Norman let go of her hand and gripped her knee as he shifted to face her. Lil's stomach twisted.

"*Our* plans?" Lil smirked.

He cleared his throat and adjusted his glasses. "I just assumed—"

"I'm joking, Norman. Just joking. I wouldn't mind doing something lowkey together. Something..."

"Discreet?" he finished her sentence for her.

"I'm sorry, Norman. It's just—"

"I get it, I do." He sighed. "You had a whole other life before I came along. And I came along at the wrong time."

"There's never a good time for a funeral director to enter the picture," Lil pointed out, only half serious.

A sad smile spread across his mouth. "The soul-crushing truth," he mumbled. "But seriously, what's the worst that can happen if we go out?"

Lil looked at him questioningly.

"I mean, so we go to dinner. We get drinks. So people see us. People we *know*. So what?"

Lil gave him a look. "We've been *through* this, Norm. You *know* what. You've just been through the wringer with Nancy. You saw what she's capable of."

"Give me one night. Just one night. New Year's Eve. If all goes well, we do it again. If not, we lay low. You have my word," Norman promised, his voice earnest.

"Okay," Lil agreed. "Maybe a movie?"

"Let's see what's playing," Norman suggested, sliding the paper from the coffee table toward himself.

Lil scooted back into the cushions of the love seat to give him room to open it.

He flipped to the "This and That" section, the front of which housed the comics, and the insides of which offered horoscope readings, the weekly police briefs, and half a page dedicated to op-eds.

Something caught Lil's attention on the inside half page.

An editorial piece. The byline?

Nancy Shytle.

LIL CALLED Betsy and Emily back into the living room, and they all pored over the scathing paragraphs.

Scathing, only inasmuch as the implications hit too close to home. Too close to Lil.

Betsy cleared her throat and read aloud from the paper for all to hear exactly what Nancy was up to.

"'Local law enforcement refuses death inquisition.'" Betsy's eyes flashed up after reading the headline.

Norman snorted. "Since when do op-eds get headlines?"

Lil paled, and her stomach churned as she nibbled her lower lip. Emily gripped her hand from her spot on the floor, sitting Indian-style at the corner of the sofa.

"G'head, Betsy. Read the damn thing," Lena spat.

Betsy rolled her shoulders back and down. "'Recently, Gull's Landing lost one of its own. A hard-working everyman by the name of Samuel Gulch.'" Betsy's eyes widened accordingly, and Lil shook her head miserably.

"Go on," she urged her friend. "Get it over with."

Betsy looked as sick as Lil felt, but she read on. "'Sam, who spent years working in the mines and mills around this state and in Pennsylvania, too, retired from that form of manual labor to move to his dream locale: down the shore in Gull's Landing, where he took up work as a house painter in the seventies. Sam didn't only work hard. He enjoyed life, too. He made friends everywhere he went, from the boardwalk to the beach, from the pier and Gull's Landing gambling hall. Everyone knew Sam.

"'That's why, when he turned sick in September of this year—an expedited sickness that attacked every last one of Sam's systems, his friends were surprised. Sam had been the picture of health before September. He was always one to join a group for drinks or take a stroll down First Street with a friend in need. To hear—through the *grapevine*, mind you—that he was suddenly and viciously sick shocked those people who loved Sam and whom Sam loved. The whole thing felt like one, big mystery.

"'And though the sickness moved fast, turning Sam ill in early September, his death was slow. According to a local source, Sam suffered in agony, dying in his home for over a month because his body couldn't take the attack. It gave up on him, although Sam's closest friends know that he surely didn't quit fighting.

"'When I set about inquiring into the death of my dear friend, Sam Gulch, I learned another thing, too. The police never insisted upon an autopsy. Despite his mystery disease and sudden disappearance from society, they laid that poor man to rest without telling Sam's friends what had happened to him. And although I refuse to perpetuate baseless rumors and water the so-called town grapevine, I hope that the good people of Gull's Landing will support me in standing up for the innocents who live among us. Be they children, women, or even kind, generous, hard-working men like Sam Gulch.'"

"I think I might be sick," Lil stood and rushed to the restroom, leaving the others to review the sinister essay.

When she returned, ashen and weak, their faces were blank. Empty. Even Norman seemed at a loss for words, despite the fact that he *knew* the details. He *knew* the story.

"I'm so sorry, Lil," Betsy whispered as Lil resumed her seat.

A mirthless laugh crawled up her throat. "Sorry for what? That Sam had an affair?"

No one dared speak a word.

"That's the gist, right? And it supports the theory I've heard here and there. You know the one—that I killed him because he was stepping out on me. At least it's coming from Nancy Shytle, though. The other offender. That should lessen the blow, right?"

"Lil," Betsy murmured, her voice low and expression inscrutable.

Lil snapped. "What? You expect me to lie down and take *that*? What does she want to do? Have him exhumed? Have his organs dug out? To prove I killed him?"

"They said he was poisoned. That's all anyone heard.

And no one *knew* you, except that you lived in the little house off the boardwalk and read Tarot cards. Rumors circulated naturally. Everyone was curious. Sam was *young*, Lil," Betsy pled.

"Are you defending her?" Lil asked, bewildered. She looked at Emily, whose face had broken into anxiety.

Lena and Irma sat quietly on the sofa, but Lena's mouth was wrinkled into the shape of a raisin, pinched and small. It was maybe the first time Lil had ever seen *her* at a loss for words.

Betsy rushed to answer. "Defending *Nancy*? No!" she cried. "I'm defending *myself*!"

"Yourself?" Lil was entirely bewildered. "Against what?"

Betsy shook her head and pressed her hands to her cheeks. "Lil, I didn't *mean* to. It just—the phone tree and then someone said Sam was poisoned. We were all confused. All of us. No one meant any harm. Until *now*." The last word came on a whisper, but by then, Lil wasn't listening.

"Back up," she demanded. "It was... *you*? *You* were the one who started the rumor that I killed Sam?"

"It was just a rumor. It didn't start that way at all. All I relayed was that the cause of his death was a secret. Lil, come on. Do you really think I believe you poisoned your husband? Do you really think *anyone* believes that?"

"Well if they didn't before, they sure as hell do now," Lena declared.

Lil groaned and paced the floor. "Sam *was* poisoned," she said. "But *I* didn't poison him. And his doctors *know* that. Norman knows, too. He was *there*. And I told him everything that happened."

"If you didn't poison him, Lil," Emily interjected, "What exactly *did* happen?"

"Lead poisoning. They didn't know if it was from the mine or from painting houses—it was bad. Very bad. He was too sick to have visitors and even if he weren't, what then? Do you think I was about to invite the likes of his *girlfriend* into our home to prove to her that Sam's disease was his own? Separate from me and my apparently distasteful reputation around town." Lil's eyes remained dry as she spoke. There was no emotion there. No love lost, even. Not in the romantic sense. Or even the familiar or friendly sense. Not anymore. And that was the problem. That Nancy had never seen those early tears that Lil had shed. The *only* ones she had shed. Nancy saw that Lil could pick up the remains of her life and move on. *Live* on.

Nancy knew Lil could live without Sam.

And Lil knew Nancy *couldn't*.

CHAPTER 35—LIL

L il pulled one, lone cigarette from a silver case and drew it to her lips, her hands trembling as she sat at a small corner table in Maeve's.

It would be the last cigarette she'd ever smoke. After this one, after she'd resolved the Nancy problem, she'd never have cause for another. With Sam dead and buried and Norman ready to sweep Lil into a blissful love affair, she wouldn't need the nasty habit to keep her from fidgeting. Her life would finally be full. She'd finally be released.

But first, she had to deal with Nancy.

Once and for all.

"Hello, Lil." Nancy passed her coat to the hostess, who took it for her as she slid onto the seat. She plucked the menu from the table, casually, as though she and Lil got together on a regular basis.

For her part, Lil slapped her menu on the table with her free hand and flicked ashes into the tray at the center. "Cigarette?" She offered the silver case to Nancy.

"I don't smoke." Nancy made a face.

"Neither do I," Lil replied smoothly, taking another drag. "Let's cut the crap, Nancy. You posted a call to action in the paper that the local law enforcement had better investigate Sam's death. You did that *knowing*—because I'm *certain* you knew that his doctor had diagnosed him— that it would go *nowhere*."

Nancy took a careful sip of her water, her long, French-tipped nails clinking on the glass. "I did *not* know what his diagnosis was. All I knew was that he was poisoned, Lillian. And neither you nor anyone else cleared the air. You never sent word across town about what happened to poor Sam. You showed up to his funeral, your eyes dry behind your black sunglasses, and you flirted with Norman Grimwood. *That's* what I know." Her voice was acid, but her red lips quivered.

"Why do you care what happened to Sam, Nancy?" There it was. The truth was all that was left. Nancy had to confess her sins right there, to Lil. She had to *break*. To confess that she'd had an affair with Sam and that ever since his death she had taken up plotting the social demise of the wife who had "killed" him. And if Nancy didn't confess, then Lil knew what she'd have to do.

She'd have to go to the newspaper, too. She'd have to stoop. She'd have to write her own scathing op-ed about a local villain, dead set on seeing the good townspeople of Gull's Landing fail in life. *And* in the hereafter.

But Nancy surprised her. Surprised Lil to the *core*.

"I did love him." Her facade broke, and tears brimmed in her eyes. "I loved Sam. Very much. But it went *nowhere*, Lillian. I can assure you of that."

"What are you talking about?" Lil demanded, nausea crawling up her throat.

"Sam wanted everything from me—he did. But I refused unless he divorced you. That was the plan. That he'd ask you for a divorce." Her voice was flat and lifeless and so unlike Nancy that Lil narrowed her gaze on the woman as if to suss out an imposter. But, no. It was Nancy, all right. A shaken, empty shell of the woman who'd fought to build a second cemetery. Who'd taken to writing a libelous, slanderous article for the paper that would put Lil in jeopardy of becoming exactly what people suspected she was: an evil wife with a flair for the wicked. A murderess.

"Why would you do this, Nancy? How does it serve you to ruin my name in the paper? It won't bring him back. It won't condemn me. I didn't *do* anything."

"You didn't *love* him enough," Nancy hissed, her character returning, her eyes on fire. "All Sam wanted was a woman's love, and you couldn't give him that."

"But you could?" Lil spat back, leaning across the table, her voice a low rumble.

"I *could*, but I *wouldn't*. Sure, we met. Clandestinely. Inappropriately, perhaps. But it never went further."

"Why do you continue to attack me? Why are you haunting me, Nancy?" Lil shot back.

"Because you *did* kill him. You didn't work, Lil. He had to. He had to work so hard to keep you two in that pretty beach house with the high taxes. And you just sat in there, doing magic and sulking around in your bathing suit."

Lil sank back into her seat.

Shock ran through her veins, but she managed a reply. An honest, heartsick reply. "You're right."

Nancy frowned. "What?"

"You're right," Lil whispered. She stubbed out her cigarette and took a long swig of water, swishing it through her mouth, suddenly repulsed by herself, itching to crawl out of her skin. To be a different person. To start life over.

But she couldn't. All she could do was agree with this horrid homewrecker... but then... had there even been a home to wreck?

"Why the second cemetery, Nancy? Why write the article?"

"The gambling hall is in trouble," Nancy replied lamely. "People are leaving town in droves to head for brighter pastures. Atlantic City. Wildwood. There are better casinos. Prettier women. Flashier venues. We can't keep up."

"And you thought erecting a cemetery would save your bottom line?" Lil shook her head, confused.

"When I went to Sam's funeral, I saw how cramped it was. This town *does* need a second cemetery. And I knew it would be a sure bet. Regardless of splitting profits, it could keep me here," Nancy replied. "But now?" She leaned forward, lacing her fingers on the tabletop. "Now, I'm not so sure that I want to stay."

"Why? Because the so-called love of your life has died?"

"That, yes," Nancy admitted. "And money. Roy is useless, if you didn't notice. He's not a provider. Not like Sam was."

It was another stab at Lil, but this time, she took it, cowering to the blow. Accepting it. Sam *was* a provider. That was true. He was a lot of things. Surely Nancy knew. "Sam was unfaithful. I didn't know it for sure until that article, though."

"Why didn't you leave? If you suspected he was unfaithful, why didn't you leave him?"

Nancy's question was fair, Lil had to give her that.

"What would I have done? Gone home to Philly? A disappointment to my family? I'd already disappointed them once when I couldn't have children. A divorce? In the sixties, when I first suspected? The seventies, when I grew surer? Even now, I'd be cast out from my own family. It wasn't like I had a back-up plan. I didn't have someone else. I didn't have *anyone*. All I had were the summers. My nieces come visit me in the summers. It's worth everything, Nancy."

"And you were willing to take Sam's mistreatment just to have the summers?"

"I didn't know for sure. Like I said, not until I read the paper—your desperate plea."

"You were wrong, though. Sam and I—we were friends. Nothing more. That killed me, mind you. But that was it. Friends. What if you were wrong? What if he was only friends with whoever else?"

"I never thought Sam was indecent, Nancy," Lil corrected.

"What? But you just said—"

"Oh, sure. He went out and about around the town. He left me home on weekend nights. He had friends by the droves. Women friends. So forth. But I never took him for a playboy. Not even an outright cheater. The problem with me and Sam, Nancy, wasn't that he slept with other women. It was that whatever he needed—a friend to confide in, a friend to enjoy a round of poker with, a friend to go for drinks—that friend was never me."

Nancy's face fell. She swallowed. Her nostrils flared and she averted her gaze to her glass of water before returning it to Lil. "I didn't know."

"Of course not. You didn't live with him. You didn't know that he'd rather be anywhere other than home. You just figured he'd rather be with you. And if Roy is as bad as Sam was, then... I suppose I can understand." Lil offered a weak smile to Nancy Shytle, her anxiety rushing out, leaving her wan and tired. "Even if I wasn't in love with Sam, I did love him, Nancy. Even if I was able to move on, which I am, I was his wife. He was my husband."

"I'm sorry, Lil," Nancy murmured, her red lips looking suddenly thinner. The chipping nail polish on her fingertips suddenly coming into Lil's focus. "I am sorry. For Sam. For the cemetery." She dipped her voice low. "*For the article.*"

"I forgive you, Nancy. Of course I forgive you," Lil answered, shaking her head to herself and standing from the table. "But really, if anything, I should be thanking you."

"Thanking me?" Nancy asked, bewildered.

"You gave me purpose. You gave me a new life, in your own twisted, unwitting way." A wry smile crept across Lil's mouth. "You gave me what I have now." Lil turned to go but remembered something else. "One more thing, Nancy."

The woman looked guiltily up at Lil. "Yes?"

"How did you get away with what you wrote? How did you get it into the paper?"

"I invest in the Gazette," Nancy answered. "I can publish almost anything I want."

"With impunity?" Lil pressed.

Nancy shrugged.

"In the spring, you'll come to the new cemetery. You'll write another op-ed, and your article will glow. And if it's good—if it's *really* nice—then maybe you can have what you were looking for all these years. The same thing Sam was looking for. The thing I, somehow, despite it all, have managed to find."

"And what's that?" Nancy asked, her eyes twinkling now with a newly forming understanding.

Lil smiled. "True friends."

EPILOGUE

O n a warm day smackdab in the middle of May, Gull's Landing buried one of its own. After a year battling lung cancer, Irma Grimwood succumbed to the disease in her home, surrounded by loved ones.

The funeral was held in Gull's Landing's recently opened graveyard. It is here, nestled between St. Gertrude's and the sprawling inland forest of New Jersey, where new life and old, new headstones and old, sprout up through the green grass together.

As part of Norman Grimwood's vision for the burial ground, plants and flowers of many varieties decorate the property. Thick, lush shrubs stand sentinel at the iron gates, gates crawling over in pretty, deep green ivy. Herbs and vegetables grow in planters that frame each row, reminiscent of Victory Gardens from the war. Though many would argue there is no victory in death, Mr. Grimwood and his sponsorship club argue otherwise. The Garden Guild is an intimate group of friends who tend the flowers and plants as part of their pledge to make their budding club a useful one.

Betsy Borden, president of the club and investor to Grimwood's mortuary business, says, "Flowers and plants represent many things to many people. We use them to celebrate and to mourn. They can be healing, and they can be toxic. Our motto in the Garden Guild is 'use the power of foliage for good.' And why not grow Christmas trees in a cemetery? Why not bring to life bushes of lavender? I know when it's my time, I can only hope that instead of being surrounded by silk flowers, I'll be surrounded by life." She tells me this as she squeezes the hand of her beau, Mr. Bill Turner, Esquire. "And in life," Betsy adds, "I want to be surrounded by love." Ms. Borden and Mr. Turner are due to be married in an intimate ceremony on the beach later this year. The bride's mother will serve as her matron of honor, and the groom's neighbor (and Lena Borden's date), Greg Rosen, will serve as the best man.

Lillian Gulch, the visionary behind the new cemetery and Mr. Grimwood's right-hand woman, tells the Gazette, "In a small town, funerals are fraught with extra meaning. Rumors swirl against the backdrop of the death of someone everyone knew. The grief is inescapable, and if the services can offer extra comfort, then they should. The Garden Guild has been around for a while in this town, but it's yet to serve as great a purpose as it does now."

When asked what that purpose is, Lil replied, "To commemorate our best friends."

Indeed, Irma Grimwood left behind several friends, if her funeral is any indicator. Not only did she have the affections of the above listed ladies, so too had Irma enchanted and befriended a new girl in town, Second Street Mortuary's own intern, Miss Emily Addams, of Wildwood. Recently divorced, Emily has started her life fresh in Gull's Landing with the help of the Garden Guild's warm welcome and Norman Grim-wood's grace.

Emily says, "Irma became like a grandmother to me. And though I only knew her for a few short months, her love proved to me that there is good in this world. In the face of all the bad that comes at a person in life, there is good, too. Good people. Good friends. Friends who are less friends and more, well, family."

With that final thought, after the lowering of the casket and the final prayer and the watering of a beautiful rosemary bush that will sit just to the side of Irma's headstone, the mourners each took a handful of earth and sprinkled it over the top of the polished, heavy wood coffin. But not Emily. Instead of a handful of earth, she released a beautiful silk scarf and watched it float down into the earthen chamber.

And thus was the first funeral to take place in Gull's Landing's newest graveyard, The Garden Cemetery.

BETSY LOOKED up from the newspaper, sighing wistfully at Nancy as they sat at their usual table at Maeve's.

Lil rose her glass of sherry. "To Irma," she said. "May she rest in peace."

"To Irma," the others murmured. Emily lifted her lemonade. Betsy, her Arnold-Palmer. Lena, wine. And, Nancy, a glass of rosé. And even Pam, who had made it back, lifted up her cocktail.

The six of them each took a modest sip, and then Lena spoke up. "I can't believe you included Betsy's nuptial plans."

"Why?" Nancy asked, bemused by the older woman.

"It's *tacky!*" Lena cried.

"Oh, *Ma*," Betsy butted in. "Who cares? If I croak and you four scheme up a sappy article that gives an update on everyone's whereabouts and dealings, well, I for one would be happy. It goes back to what we believe as a *club*."

"And what's that?" Lil asked.

"Life and death—they go hand in hand," Emily offered. She adjusted the silk scarf around her neck, a matching accessory to the one she'd buried with her dear friend.

"So, what's next?" Betsy asked, changing the subject as their lunch arrived. After the funeral the preceding week, there had been a modest reception for Irma—in her home. Nancy had run her review of the cemetery, as she'd promised Lil when they had come to their agreement the previous winter. Although it was more a review of Irma's ceremony, naturally. But that was a good thing, truly.

Afterwards, the women had agreed to have their next meeting of the Garden Guild at Maeve's, like old times. But now, they'd start planning for the future in earnest. What with all of their spring blooms coming up and more work to do at the new cemetery than ever, they were busy, busy, busy.

Having so much to do had helped them re-integrate Nancy into the group. The girls warmed to her over time, coming to accept Betsy's advice about when to choose anger and when to choose forgiveness. That advice had helped Emily to move on, too. Enough so that she'd spent

Easter with her father and stepmother. A brief brunch, she'd called it, but it was pleasant enough that she might go home again from time to time.

As for Nancy, with Bill's help, she had secured a congenial divorce with Roy. Because they had split their assets evenly—and therefore their various business engagements—Nancy knew she had to take up a new project. Something to keep her occupied.

"I'm planting pumpkins," Lil announced. "And then I need to start getting ready for the girls to come this summer. They'll be here in a month, if you can believe that."

Emily added, "I have to take summer coursework to keep pace with my program, but Norman says he can help here and there, and it looks like I'll be able to get a raise soon, too."

"That's great, Emily," Betsy said.

"Greg is taking me to Maine for a week. I don't know *why*, but there you have it. People will talk. I just *know* it. People will talk. Especially now with that *fluff* piece of yours, Nancy." Lena lifted an eyebrow.

Nancy smiled good-naturedly, and Betsy turned to look at her mother, "At least they aren't saying you killed your husband."

Lil rolled her eyes. "How about you, Betsy?"

"Well, the wedding, naturally. After that, more business, I hope. I think I'm on a roll, you know. Taking over Nancy's old territory in having a hand in so many local businesses, I suppose. Sorry, Nanc." Betsy winked at Nancy.

"How's the new job, Nancy?" Lil asked. Since the

divorce, Nancy had taken up as a local journalist with the Gull's Landing Gazette. It suited her, spreading the good —and the bad—word about town. And it had helped to ignite her friendship with Lil. Or, helped to nurture the friendship into being, at the very least. Under her new appointment with the *Gazette*, Nancy had tastefully and masterfully absolved the questions she'd raised about Sam by publishing a series about the workplace and in-home dangers of lead paint exposure.

"I'm doing an investigative piece, actually. Norman brought it to my attention."

"Oh?" Betsy asked, swirling her drink before sipping it.

"Yes, someone called to report another vagrant death, and the county brought the remains to the new cemetery. Norman says he'll continue to use the extra space in the early part of the Garden—the old potter's field—to bury him. Another benefit, I suppose."

"Where did they find the body?" Emily asked, her eyebrows knitted together in either fear or repulsion.

"That's what I'm looking into," Nancy replied. "It's this old house out on Mill River Road."

"Out in the country?" Lil asked, referring to the back-roads of town that ran along Mill River.

"Yes, a little house in the country. It's not so little, actually. It's a bit of a mansion. A run down, country house, I suppose. That's where they found him."

"Whose house is it?" Lil pressed, intrigued.

Nancy pursed her lips. "It was just recently bequeathed to the daughter of the original owners. Preston is her name, I believe. Meryl Preston."

LEARN MORE about Meryl Preston and the Mill River country house. Order *The Country Club* today.

Keep up to date with news and releases, join Elizabeth Bromke's newsletter by visiting her website, elizabethbromke.com.

Looking for a series to get lost in? Check out the best-selling saga, *Birch Harbor.*

ALSO BY ELIZABETH BROMKE

Birch Harbor:

House on the Harbor

Lighthouse on the Lake

Fireflies in the Field

Cottage by the Creek

Bells on the Bay

Gull's Landing:

The Summer Society, a USA Today Bestseller

The Garden Guild

The Country Club

Harbor Hills:

The House on Apple Hill Lane

The Hickory Grove Series

ACKNOWLEDGMENTS

The Garden Guild was a fun project. Lena particularly sort of just fell out of my brain, splatting onto the computer screen. She made me laugh out loud sometimes! I often draw inspiration for my characters from those near and dear to me, such as my grandmothers, Dorothy Rita and Jeanette. I love you both! Do you see yourselves in these pages? Because you're *here*.

As always, I am so grateful to Elise Griffin of Edits with Elise for your skillful examination of the story *and* mechanics. Also, to Lisa Lee—thank you for always being "at the ready." Thank you both. Any errors in this book are mine alone or intentional.

Wilette Cruz of Red Leaf Book Design: another winner! Thank you for your hard work, incredible artistry, and professionalism. I'm so blessed Rachael brought us together!

My early reader team is like my cocoon. Huge thanks to the lovely ladies who take my book babies early, read them, send me their thoughts, and share those thoughts with the world. I appreciate you all so much!

These past few months have challenged me a great deal. With the return to school and the pressures of life in this new normal, I couldn't be more thankful for having such a strong support system on the home front. Dad, Mom, Ed, and Eddie—thank you for all your patience with me. I love you all so much! Eddie, you are my reason!

And now, onto the next one!

ABOUT THE AUTHOR

After graduating from the University of Arizona, Elizabeth Bromke became an English teacher. You can still find her in a classroom today, behind a stack of essays and a leaning tower of classic novels.

When she's not teaching, Elizabeth writes women's fiction and contemporary romance. For fun, she enjoys jigsaw puzzles, crosswords, and—of course—reading.

Elizabeth lives in the northern mountains of Arizona with her husband, son, and their sweet dog Winnie.

Learn more about the author by visiting her website at elizabethbromke.com.